THE MARK OF THE BEAST

The Mark of the Beast

LEFT BEHIND

>THE KIDS<

Jerry B. Jenkins

Tim LaHaye

WITH CHRIS FABRY

TYNDALE
KIDS

TYNDALE HOUSE PUBLISHERS, INC.
WHEATON, ILLINOIS

Visit Tyndale's exciting Web site at www.tyndale.com

Discover the latest Left Behind news at www.leftbehind.com

Published in association with the literary agency of Alive Communications, Inc., 7680 Goddard Street, Suite 200, Colorado Springs, CO 80920.

Edited by Curtis H. C. Lundgren

ISBN 0-8423-5792-0, mass paper

Printed in the United States of America

08 07 06 05 04 03
9 8 7 6 5 4 3 2 1

b1318642

To Todd and Julie

TABLE OF CONTENTS

What's Gone On Before

JUDD Thompson Jr. and the rest of the Young Tribulation Force are living the adventure of a lifetime. Judd and Lionel Washington watch in amazement as Nicolae Carpathia comes back from the dead. When the surrounding crowd worships the potentate, Judd and Lionel go separate ways.

Global Community Peacekeepers discover Vicki Byrne and the other kids hiding in Wisconsin. Vicki and Darrion Stahley run, but they get locked inside the trunk of a GC car and ride toward Des Plaines, Illinois. Mark Eisman and the rest of the group are threatened by a raging wildfire in Lake Geneva and discover new friends who have an underground hideout.

Vicki and Darrion escape the GC and find an older believer, Maggie Carlson, who helps them communicate with Natalie, a friend working inside the Global Community.

Lionel searches for Judd in New Babylon

and finds him in a medical tent recovering from an accident. The two return to their hotel room, where the lead singer for The Four Horsemen, Z-Van, is busy writing songs that celebrate Nicolae Carpathia's triumph over death. Though they both want to go home to their friends, Judd and Lionel feel drawn to Israel.

Vicki's friend, Natalie Bishop, tricks her GC superior and seizes a chance to help the kids escape.

Join the Young Tribulation Force as they work together and prepare for the deadly mark of the beast.

ONE

The Getaway

VICKI mashed the accelerator to the floor and glanced in the rearview mirror. Flashing lights from an oncoming Global Community squad car cast an eerie glow in the rain. A shadowy figure darted across the wet street. *Natalie should have come with us,* Vicki thought.

Charlie craned his neck to see, and Vicki told him to stay down.

"You think they're going to shoot at us?" Darrion said.

Vicki shrugged. "Just stay down."

Phoenix squirmed in the backseat. Charlie grabbed his collar and pulled him to the floor. "He's excited to see you!"

"I'll be excited to see him once we get away," Vicki said, gripping the steering wheel. She kept the lights off, hoping the GC car wouldn't spot them in the rain. Vicki's heart raced so fast she found it hard to breathe.

She remembered the driving instructions Conrad had given during their trip west. "Make sure you stay calm behind the wheel," Conrad had said. "If you're angry or scared, don't drive."

"Great," Vicki had said. "I'll never learn because I'm always angry or scared."

Conrad had helped Vicki get comfortable with driving in all kinds of weather. During a severe rainstorm in California, she drove in an empty parking lot, sliding when she made sharp turns. Now, as she rushed down the wet road, the practice was paying off.

"Where are we going?" Charlie said.

Vicki quickly explained about the kids in Wisconsin. "We may not make it tonight, but we'll try." She turned a corner without touching her brakes and grazed a parked car.

"They're stopping at Maggie's house," Darrion yelled.

Vicki drove on, wondering what Natalie would say to her boss.

Natalie Bishop leaned against the car, rain dripping from her hair, as Deputy Commander Darryl Henderson stumbled down Maggie Carlson's front steps. He fell in the wet grass with a thump.

Natalie screamed in mock pain. She quickly reached into Henderson's car, stuffed his keys in her pocket, and kept screaming. She fumbled with her key chain—a combination pocketknife, flashlight, and Mace dispenser.

Natalie had seen a few prisoners who had been maced. Their eyes turned red and filled with tears. She could only imagine the pain.

"Bishop!" Deputy Commander Henderson shouted. The man was on his feet again. "Bishop, what happened?"

Natalie pulled the Mace dispenser close as lights swirled from the oncoming GC squad car. She glanced at the car Vicki was driving and saw it move around a corner.

This is my only hope, Natalie thought. She had planned it this way, and so far everything was working. Vicki and the others were gone, and if Henderson believed her, she might be able to keep working for the GC.

"Where are they?" Henderson screamed as he opened the car door.

Natalie closed her eyes tightly, pressed the nozzle, then opened them as the spray filled her eyes. For several moments she could hear nothing but her own screams. Unbelievable, searing pain! Her eyes felt on fire. She covered her face with her hands and rolled on the pavement, unable to focus on anything but the pain.

"Where are my keys!?" Henderson said.

Another GC squad car pulled up, and an officer tried to help Natalie. Henderson screamed for the man to follow the car that had just pulled away.

"I didn't see any—"

The officer sped off and Henderson barked orders into his radio. An older woman arrived, and Henderson questioned her about her car. She gave him the information, and he called for all available units to respond.

The woman knelt by Natalie and asked what was wrong. Natalie said she had been sprayed with Mace, and the woman helped her into the house. "We need to flush your eyes with water."

As Henderson combed the yard for his keys, the woman took Natalie to the kitchen. "That was a brave thing you did for those kids," she whispered.

Natalie tried to open her eyes but couldn't.

"It's okay," the woman said. "I can see by the mark on your forehead that you're a believer. I'm Maggie Carlson."

Natalie sobbed, forced to her knees by the pain. "I took Henderson's car keys so he couldn't follow," she whispered. "If he finds them—"

"Where are they?"

Natalie patted her right pants pocket and Maggie took them out. "I'll care for them. Keep your eyes under the running water."

Judd Thompson Jr. sat alone on a leather couch in Z-Van's hotel suite and prayed for his friends. He had sensed danger several times before, but never so strong as now.

As the New Babylon sun peeked over the palace a few blocks away, Judd took a bottle of water from the small refrigerator and walked into the main living area. Z-Van's sheet music lay stacked on the grand piano, but Judd couldn't look at the words. The man had seemed possessed since the day Carpathia had risen from the dead, spending every waking moment writing his tribute to the risen potentate. Judd knew Nicolae could take power over people's minds. Was Carpathia controlling the singer?

Judd used a laptop to log on to the kids' Web site. He read Tsion Ben-Judah's latest message again and shuddered at the prophecies about the Antichrist. Soon the Global Community would require every living being to receive a mark on the hand or forehead and swear allegiance to Carpathia. Anyone who willingly took that evil mark would never be able to come to God.

That's why we have to tell as many people as quickly as we can, Judd thought.

Around the world, loyal citizens were prepared to kneel before Carpathia's image. The GC had been working on biochip technology that would accompany the mark, but Judd didn't know how long it would take to distribute the machines used for the injection.

Judd thought of the trip Z-Van had planned to Jerusalem. It would be safer to hide or get out of New Babylon altogether. But something in Israel tugged at him. Was it Sam? Mr. Stein? Nada's family? Lionel felt it too, so they had stayed.

Judd typed a short note to his friends in the Young Tribulation Force and asked about everyone. He knew Charlie had been taken by the GC and wondered if this was the reason he felt the need to pray.

Judd was astounded at the number of e-mails to the Web site. He had known when they started it that many would read its contents, but he had no idea hundreds of kids would e-mail every day from around the globe. They asked everything from how to become a true believer to what was coming next on the prophecy timeline. Mark and the others had done a good job of listing the most frequently asked questions, or FAQs, but some wanted a personal response.

One girl from the former country of France gave a first name of Eleta and wrote:

> *I grew up knowing nothing about God. My parents and teachers never talked about spiritual things, believing religion was unimportant or just superstitious. Now that Nicolae Carpathia and Leon Fortunato have performed miracles, many are saying Carpathia is truly a god. They want to worship him, but I'm not sure. The things you have posted make me wonder if Carpathia is really evil. Please help me understand the truth so that I can tell my family.*

Judd's heart leapt. This was exactly the kind of person the kids had hoped to reach. Judd sent a message, quickly explaining more about what the Bible revealed about God and how important it was to not follow the Global Community's twisted religion.

Sadly, others wrote in support of Carpathia. One man said he was monitoring the Web site and had notified local GC authorities. *It's only a matter of time until they find you and shut you down!*

Judd heard someone stir in the next room. He started to leave the Web site, but a new message sparked his interest. The subject line read *New Babylon believer—help.*

Lionel walked into the room with Westin Jakes, Z-Van's pilot who had become a believer. Judd waved them over and put the e-mail onto the full screen.

> *Dear Young Trib Force,*
>
> *I am seventeen and a believer in Jesus. I have been visiting New Babylon with my parents. My father is a huge supporter of N. C. and came to pay his respects at the funeral. He and my mother do not know of my faith in Christ.*
>
> *My father wants me to work for the GC. Though I'm still in high school, I have a number of skills with computers. The GC have given us a free apartment until I can be processed for employment.*
>
> *The last thing I want to do is work for the Global Community, but my father insists. We have had arguments and he will not listen. Me working for Carpathia is an honor greater than anything my father can imagine. Can you help me? I have only two believers I can talk to right now. Please write as soon as possible.*
>
> *C. W.*

Lionel studied the message. "You think it's a trick?"

"Looks genuine to me," Westin said.

Judd nodded and typed a reply. "I think this is someone in a real jam."

"We have no idea who this C. W. is," Lionel said.

"Doesn't matter. If he's a fellow believer, he deserves our help."

"What advice are you going to give him— or her?"

Judd smiled. "No advice. I'm going to set up a meeting."

Vicki made her way through backstreets and alleys, trying to stay out of sight. A few minutes after they had escaped, she took a wrong turn down a dead end. As they turned the car around, a GC squad car passed on the street in front of them, its lights flashing.

"Maybe we ought to find a place to hide," Darrion said.

Vicki shook her head. "The GC will be crawling all over here by morning. It's dark and raining. We should try to get as far away as we can."

Lightning struck nearby and the sky thundered. Phoenix whimpered in the backseat and Charlie tried to comfort him.

With their lights still off, Vicki found what was left of Rand Road and headed north. Anytime she saw the lights of GC squad cars, she turned at the nearest street and stayed out of sight.

Charlie leaned forward. "When are we going back for Bo and Ginny?"

Vicki stole a glance at Darrion. "Natalie couldn't get to the Shairtons."

"You mean we're just going to leave them?"

Darrion turned in the seat. "We need to get you to safety, and then we'll see about them."

"I don't want to get to safety. I want to help them. They were like a mom and dad to me. Can we turn around?"

Vicki shook her head. "I don't expect you to understand, Charlie. We need to keep going."

Charlie slumped in his seat and put his face in his hands. Lightning flashed and Vicki spotted a sign that said "Wauconda." Several headlights approached from behind. A few miles later, Darrion spotted a street sign and asked Vicki to turn. They followed a muddy road into the countryside.

When they reached what looked like an

old general store, Vicki parked in the back. With each flash of lightning they spotted abandoned barns, cornfields, and old farm equipment.

Vicki fished Maggie's cell phone from her pocket and called Mark in Wisconsin. He was glad to hear they were safe and asked about Natalie. Mark offered to meet them, but Vicki said they would keep driving and call again before daybreak.

The three sat in the car, staring out at the darkness. The only sounds were the patter of raindrops on the roof and Phoenix panting. Finally, Darrion broke the silence. "My mom and dad used to bring me up here every fall to pick apples. I wish I could get a mug of hot apple cider right now."

Vicki smiled. "Or a caramel apple." She turned and put a hand on Charlie's shoulder. "It's good to have you back."

"Didn't think I was going to get out."

Vicki scooted down in her seat. "Tell me more about picking apples."

"My dad would hold me on his shoulders so I could get the high ones. Then I'd find the biggest pumpkin, and he'd carry it back to the car."

"Petting zoo?" Vicki said.

"How'd you know?"

"One of our neighbors knew a farm family. I always liked the hayrides."

"The place we went to had a corn maze. They'd cut rows out of a cornfield and you'd have to try and find your way to the middle."

Vicki thought of her little sister, Jeanni. Just the sight of cows by the side of the road made the girl squeal with delight. Vicki closed her eyes and began to cry. Darrion put a hand on her shoulder.

"I'm okay," Vicki said. "I was just thinking about my sister petting those farm animals. She always laughed when she fed the goats. For some reason I can't remember her face anymore. I try hard, but . . ."

A light flashed inside a house behind them. Tears ran down Vicki's cheeks as she started the car and headed for the main road.

TWO

Roadblocks

NATALIE Bishop let the water cascade over her eyes for almost a half hour. She looked at her red, puffy face in a kitchen mirror and rubbed her eyes with a fresh towel.

Deputy Commander Henderson was picked up by another squad car to direct the search. Maggie slipped outside and put his keys under his car as another Peacekeeper came to take Natalie's statement.

"So the kid with the dog maced you and got out of the car?"

Natalie nodded.

"Wasn't he handcuffed?"

"He was, but Deputy Commander Henderson said we could take them off, just to show him we were his friends."

"And you didn't put the cuffs on after you got the call from the woman?"

Natalie rubbed her eyes. "I thought I did, but I guess he tricked me. Maybe he got the key. I can't remember."

The Peacekeeper went in the other room and talked with Maggie. Deputy Commander Henderson returned a half hour later.

"Did you catch them?" Natalie said.

Henderson shook his head and ignored her, looking around the house. He spotted the computer and asked Maggie if the girls had used it.

"They sure did. They were on it almost the whole time they were here."

Henderson turned the computer on and looked at Natalie. "You okay?"

"I'll feel better when this stuff wears off."

"I read your statement. Something's not right."

"What do you mean?" Natalie said.

Maggie brought Henderson some coffee and a sweet roll and sat at the kitchen table. "This girl has been through a lot. I don't think she's the one to blame."

"I didn't even want to stay with that guy," Natalie said. "I wanted to come with you."

Henderson scratched his chin. "Doesn't make sense. These two girls leave your house before we get here and wait? How would they know this Charlie kid is with us?" He turned to Maggie. "Tell me the truth."

"I already told you. They forced their way into the house and took over. I was so scared I hardly knew what to do. They used the computer and ate like they were starving. It was a miracle I was able to break away and call you when I did."

"And they found out you were talking to me?"

Maggie nodded. "I tried to get them to think it was a friend, but they knew I had called the GC. They grabbed my car keys and ran. What could I do?"

Henderson went back to the computer and started typing, but the machine beeped. "They must have erased the hard drive."

Maggie shook her head. "These kids are smart. Maybe they were going to steal your car. Then they saw this Charlie kid and took off."

"Maybe . . ."

"I'm sure you'll catch them eventually."

"Eventually's not good enough," Henderson said, taking a bite of the sweet roll and sipping his coffee. "I have to say you were brave, ma'am. And you're right. We will catch them. We have roadblocks set up from here to the northern border. Plus, I've asked assistance with satellite imaging."

"What's that?" Natalie said.

"GC Security and Intelligence can snap pictures from miles above the earth. If we give them the coordinates and the weather cooperates, they can detect movement and give us reports."

Maggie gave Natalie a worried look, then turned back to Henderson. "So you will catch them."

"You bet." He took another sweet roll. "And believe me, when we have them in custody, your contribution to the search will be recognized."

Maggie smiled and brought more food and coffee for the other Peacekeeper. She turned to Natalie. "Why don't you go upstairs and lie down in my room. I'm sure resting your eyes will help."

"Go ahead," Henderson said. "We'll wait on the satellite report."

Maggie patted Natalie on the back and pressed a piece of paper into her hand. When Natalie got to the top of the stairs, she opened it and found a phone number along with a note. *Call them now.*

A noise at the bottom of the stairs startled Natalie. She turned to see the other Peace-keeper looking up at her.

Mark Eisman studied the hastily drawn map Colin Dial had made of the upper Illinois/lower Wisconsin area. Vicki would need to work her way around several lakes to get to the new hideout.

"The earthquake cut off a lot of roads," Colin said, pointing to an old map. "These two lakes are dry craters, and it's impossible to get through except on foot. The GC made a main road toward Lake Geneva, but I don't think she should go that way." Colin traced a route and told Mark to call Vicki.

"She's driving blind," Mark said. "How's she going to find roads in the dark that don't even exist on a map?"

Vicki drove back to the main road and continued north. The rain had slowed, and she flashed her lights every minute to make sure she was on course.

"You think those people back there in the house will phone the GC?" Charlie said.

"I hope they'll go back to bed and forget about us."

The cell phone rang and Vicki pulled over.

"Vicki, it's Mark. We have directions to get

you here, but it's complicated. Where are you?"

Vicki told him and Mark talked with his friend, Colin Dial. "Okay, head north on Route 12. When you get to Fox Lake, which isn't there anymore, pull off and call me."

Vicki followed Mark's directions. The clouds were clearing and she could finally see moonlight.

"As long as we keep our lights off, they won't be able to see us, right?" Charlie said.

Vicki nodded.

Natalie smiled at the Peacekeeper, and the man returned to the kitchen. She slipped into Maggie's bedroom, closed the door quietly, and picked up the phone by the bed. No dial tone. It was either the storm or the GC had cut the lines. *Do they suspect Maggie?*

Natalie fell onto the bed and buried her face in a pillow. Her eyes still stung, but she couldn't think of that now. She had to figure out a way to warn Vicki. "Please, God, help me get in touch with her."

Natalie heard a commotion and went to the top of the stairs.

Deputy Commander Henderson paced as he talked on his cell phone. "That would fit," he said, covering the phone with a hand. "We just got a report from Wauconda. A suspicious car was seen outside a home. They left a few minutes ago."

Henderson put the phone back to his ear. "I don't know how they got that far, but we won't miss them this time. Give me the satellite coordinates."

Natalie went back downstairs and stood in the kitchen doorway. She gave Maggie a worried look.

"All right, I want three cars at the northern roadblock at Richmond to move south toward Wauconda," Henderson said. "We should run right into them."

Lionel Washington sensed an old feeling creeping up on him. Judd was at it again, doing what he thought was right and not caring about anyone else. Though they had fought during their time together in Israel and in New Babylon, Lionel liked Judd. It was impossible not to like him. But when Judd made up his mind, nothing and no one could stop him.

Like other mornings, Lionel went to the lobby for some food. He knew Z-Van had spent thousands of dollars on room service and Lionel could order anything he wanted, but he felt guilty eating what he considered "Carpathia food."

Lionel grabbed a tray and went through the complimentary buffet of muffins, doughnuts, fruit, cereal, and juice. People gathered around small breakfast tables and talked about the events of the past week. Nicolae's rise from the dead was replayed on wall-mounted televisions. When Leon Fortunato called down lightning on the crowd, many in the dining room clapped. All of the clips were in preparation for a live news conference at the GC Palace.

When Leon Fortunato appeared on the screen, many applauded, then called for quiet. "Hail Carpathia," Leon began.

"Hail Carpathia," people said to the television.

"I am here to outline plans our beloved potentate has put into effect in the last few days and to keep everyone abreast of the schedule we have laid out to celebrate the resurrection of our lord and risen king.

"I want you to know that I will no longer be supreme commander of the Global Community."

Many around Lionel gasped and the room fell silent.

Leon smiled. "At the potentate's request,

I have accepted, with great enthusiasm I might add, the new position of Most High Reverend Father of Carpathianism. The former Enigma Babylon One World faith will be replaced with a more perfect religion, one that worships a worthy object. That is, the one who raised himself from the dead, Nicolae Carpathia."

This was not news to Lionel. He had heard it from Z-Van, but clearly those in the room were surprised and joyful at the report.

"As has been relayed to you through news channels," Fortunato continued, "the image of His Excellency is being reproduced around the world in every major city. Each image will be a life-size replica of His Excellency.

"Let me say another word about our worthy lord. While our beloved potentate lay dead, he gave me power to call fire from the sky and kill those who oppose him. He also allowed me to give speech to the statue so we could hear his own heart. This confirmed my desire to serve him as my god for the rest of my days, and I shall do that for as long as Nicolae Carpathia gives me breath."

Leon said he would take questions from the press after one final announcement. "To further the cause of world peace and unity, the Global Community is beginning a massive identification plan that will encompass every man, woman, and child on the planet. This loyalty mark will be on a biochip embedded just beneath the skin. It will contain a series of numbers matching the world region where each person lives. There will also be a physical representation of this mark on the body."

Leon paused for what seemed like dramatic effect. The breakfast room fell silent. Even people walking through the lobby stopped to listen as Leon continued, his voice peaceful and soothing.

"Every man, woman, and child, regardless of their station in life, shall receive this mark on their right hand or on their forehead. Those who neglect to get the mark when it is made available will not be allowed to buy or sell until such time as they receive it. Those who overtly refuse shall be put to death, and every marked loyal citizen shall be deputized with the right and the responsibility to report such a one. The mark shall consist of the name of His Excellency or the prescribed number."

Lionel felt goose bumps. Fortunato had just announced the death penalty for anyone refusing the mark, but people around him seemed eager to identify with Carpathia.

A reporter raised a hand. "Sir, what is the potentate's position on those who oppose him, specifically the Jewish contingent in

Jerusalem and the Judah-ites who are spread around the globe?"

Fortunato smiled. "We believe these misguided groups will see the errors they have made when the potentate returns to Jerusalem in the beloved Holy Land. The Jews are looking for their Messiah, and Nicolae Carpathia will return there, triumphant. Each person will have an opportunity to repent and see the light.

"The Judah-ites believe Messiah already came and went. They think Jesus is their Savior." Leon seemed to look around the room. "But I see him nowhere. If the Judah-ites want to see the true and living God, let them come to Jerusalem, for that is where he shall soon be. In the city where they slew him, they shall see him, high and lifted up."

Another reporter said, "The controls that you're putting on citizens—such as the mark and the biochip—are we to conclude that citizens aren't to be trusted?"

"On the contrary. Most people believe in and follow the tenets of the Global Community. It is only that small percentage I have just mentioned who are not loyal. We seek peace and unity for all, and in order to accomplish that, all must comply."

"Ask him when we'll be able to take the

mark!" someone shouted in the breakfast room. Everyone laughed.

"If someone should choose against the loyalty mark," another reporter said, "how will they be . . . handled?"

Fortunato smiled again. "I'm sure you will agree that no thinking person would choose against allegiance to a man who has proved his divine nature by raising himself from the dead. Let us hope there will be no need to even address that question."

"How will the mark be applied?" another reporter said.

"The miniature biochip will go under the skin as painlessly as a vaccination. It takes only a matter of seconds. Citizens may choose either their hand or their forehead. The procedure will leave a thin, half-inch scar, and to its immediate left will be the home region number in black ink. Some may also choose the initials *NJC* or even the name *Nicolae* which would cover the left side of the forehead.

"The embedded chip will not only give evidence of loyalty to the potentate, but also will serve as a method of payment and receipt for buying and selling."

"When will this start?"

"We intend to implement the mark as soon as possible. First, those who are behind bars will have the opportunity to show their loyalty and then members of the Global Community workforce."

Lionel grabbed the tray of food and walked to the elevator. Fortunato could fool members of the press and other viewers, but followers of God knew what was about to happen. Those who took the mark would lose their souls for eternity. Those who didn't would lose their heads. Simple as that.

THREE

Into the Culvert

NATALIE followed Deputy Commander Henderson to the street. She pointed at something shiny under the car, and Henderson retrieved his keys.

"You're not going. Your eyes—"

"I'm fine. I need to be there when you get these jerks."

Henderson sighed and tossed his bag in the backseat. "No complaining. We're staying out as long as it takes to find them. I'm not having it on my record that I let a prisoner escape and meet up with other suspects."

"I understand, sir."

The other Peacekeeper turned on the dome light and studied a map. He pointed out the roadblock location and the Wauconda sighting.

Natalie glanced at Henderson's bag beside her, which held an extra gun, ammunition, important papers, and his cell phone. She unsnapped the phone compartment and felt inside. Empty.

Henderson started the car and handed his phone to the Peacekeeper. "Call the satellite office and see if there's anything new."

The Peacekeeper dialed the number and cursed. "We must be out of range."

"Let me try," Natalie said. "I'll keep dialing until we get through."

The Peacekeeper handed the phone to Natalie.

Vicki flashed her lights and saw the sign for Fox Lake. She pulled to the side of the road and turned off the car. Charlie had fallen asleep in the backseat beside Phoenix.

"What did Mark mean about Fox Lake not being here anymore?" Darrion said.

"I'm guessing the earthquake drained it," Vicki said. She looked at the fuel gauge and saw they still had a quarter of a tank. "We should be able to get to Wisconsin on this."

Vicki dialed Mark and told him where they were.

"Good. I'm going to let Colin give you

directions. Do you have a pen and some paper?"

Vicki fumbled in the glove box and found a pen. Darrion pulled a manual from under her seat, and Vicki wrote on the inside cover.

"Listen carefully," Colin said.

The phone beeped and the screen said "Low battery."

"Do you have a recharger?" Colin said.

"Not unless it's in the glove compartment," Vicki said.

"Look for it and call me in five minutes. I'll try to make the directions as simple as I can."

Vicki turned off the phone and crawled through the car looking for the phone cord that plugged into the cigarette lighter. Charlie slept through the futile search.

"How much time is left on the battery?" Darrion said.

"I think the warning light comes on a few minutes before it actually runs out. We should have enough power to get the directions."

Vicki turned on the phone and dialed, but before she could hit the Send button, the phone rang. She picked up and heard static.

Then someone said, "I'm not getting anything. We're still out of range."

"Who is it?" Darrion said.

"It sounds like Natalie, but—"

"How did you come up with the idea for the satellite, Mr. Henderson?"

Vicki covered the phone's mouthpiece. "It is Natalie. I think she's trying to warn us."

Henderson said something in the background. Then Natalie said, "So as soon as we get in touch with the satellite guys, we'll know their exact location?"

Vicki told Darrion what she had heard, and the phone beeped a low battery signal again.

"If they're heading north on Route 12," Natalie said, "and those three cars from the Richmond roadblock are heading south, we're sure to catch them."

Vicki whispered, "Thanks, Natalie." She punched in the number for Mark.

Colin answered and Vicki explained what she had learned. "That changes things," Colin said. "If they know your location, it won't matter how many back roads you take. Plus, you'll lead them right here."

"My battery's almost gone. What do I do?"

Colin spoke with Mark quickly and said, "Okay, see if you can find a good place to pull off the road ahead and hide. When the southbound GC cars pass you, keep going north until you get to the Richmond roadblock. Park and head out on foot. Mark and I will—"

Click.

The phone went blank. Vicki tried turning it on but it was dead. She told Darrion what Colin had said.

"About a mile back, there was a turnoff," Darrion said.

Headlights shone in the distance and Vicki gunned the engine, spinning the car around and heading south. "Just tell me when we get close."

Natalie had heard Vicki's whisper and turned the phone off. She scrolled through the directory and erased the call so Henderson wouldn't know what she had done.

When she dialed the number for the satellite station, it rang. She handed the phone to Henderson, and the man beamed.

"Give me an update. . . . Cloud cover? What's that got to do—? . . . Okay, so it's lifting now. That means you should be able to see something."

Henderson gave the satellite operator the proper coordinates and asked him to look for three cars heading south and one probably going north. Natalie sat helpless, praying for clouds and rain.

Judd told Lionel that their mysterious contact inside the palace, known as C. W., had written back almost immediately and agreed to meet in a park not far from the hotel.

Lionel shook his head. "You're walking into this blind. We should be getting out of here, not meeting people who could be GC."

"I don't know who this guy is," Judd said, "but I think he's a believer. If he's really in trouble, I want to help."

Lionel stared at the television as Leon Fortunato continued his press conference. Judd changed and headed for the door of the suite. Westin offered to drive, but Judd said he would walk. He looked back once more before he left, but Lionel simply stared at the television.

Judd left the hotel lobby and headed toward the palace. It had been almost a week since Nicolae's body had been returned to New Babylon. The city looked much different now. Gone were the people mourning in the streets and the windows draped with black curtains. Now people from around the world searched for mementos of their visit.

One booth Judd passed sold necklaces with Nicolae's name embedded in a jewel. Another offered a prayer cloth with the face of Nicolae pictured on the front. The busiest kiosk sold miniature replicas of the Carpathia statue. Judd picked one up and pushed a button on the back. A deep voice said, "Hail Carpathia, risen from the dead." Judd nearly dropped it.

As Judd made his way to the park, he noticed freshly planted trees and a new water fountain. He sat on a bench and looked at the beautiful garden. The last time he had been in the area, Nada had been waiting.

Nada.

He whispered her name and a wave of emotion swept over him. He had recently e-mailed Sam and asked him to pass along some questions to Nada's mother.

"Why did you choose the name *Nada*?" Judd had asked.

"In some countries the name means 'hope,' " Nada's mother answered. "That certainly fits her personality. She was full of hope and promise for the future. But in our part of the world the name means 'giving.' "

Judd closed his eyes. *Giving.* That definition fit as well. Nada had given her life for him, jumping in front of a jailer just as the man's gun fired. One moment she was full of life, the next she was on the floor, her breath and blood escaping like some wounded animal's.

Judd leaned forward, elbows on knees. Just

thinking about the scene in the Global Community jail took his breath away. He closed his eyes and tried to think of something else. Anything. Z-Van. Westin.

He took another breath and thought of Lionel. *Am I walking into a trap?*

Footsteps crunched on the walking path nearby. "Are you all right?" someone said.

Judd looked up. A Global Community Peacekeeper stood over him.

Vicki sped south on Route 12 with the GC cars gaining on them. She drove without lights and several times found herself careening around curves and running off the road.

"Don't use your brakes or they'll see the lights," Darrion said.

Charlie woke up as they lurched off and back on the road. "What's going on?"

"Just stay down and buckle up," Vicki said.

Charlie held Phoenix and lay across the backseat.

Vicki rounded a corner and Darrion pointed. "There it is, on the left!"

Vicki glanced in her rearview mirror. She couldn't see the lights of the oncoming GC cars, so she slammed on her brakes and turned the steering wheel to the left. The rear of the car slid around on the wet pavement. She pushed the accelerator and the car screamed down an embankment, metal scraping against dirt and rocks, then concrete. Something banged underneath as they stopped and the car rumbled loudly. Vicki pulled forward a few more feet into a clump of willows.

"That doesn't sound good," Darrion said.

Vicki turned off the car and rolled down her window. Crickets chirped in the night and she drank in the fresh, earthy smell. The three sat in silence as the hum of car tires approached from the north. Vicki turned and looked at Charlie and Phoenix. She put a finger to her lips as headlights flashed high above. Phoenix whimpered, as if he knew something was happening.

The first car passed and the second followed. Vicki listened for the squeal of brakes, but the cars continued until the whine of the tires drifted off on the wet breeze.

"They passed us!" Darrion said.

"Wait. Natalie said there were three cars coming from the north. That was only two."

"Maybe she was wrong," Charlie said.

Vicki held up a hand. In the distance, the third car approached slowly, shining a bright light on either side of the road. "This guy is going to see us if he's going that slow."

"Quick," Darrion said, "everybody out and cover the top!"

The kids got out, making sure Phoenix stayed in the backseat. The girls grabbed leaves, sticks, and even chunks of earth and threw it all on top of the car. Charlie grabbed armloads of dead willow branches and scattered them on the roof. Near a huge drain Vicki found piles of tin cans and trash. She scooped it all up and frantically threw it on the hood and trunk.

"He's getting close!" Darrion whispered.

Charlie put one more armload of branches on the side of the car and followed the girls into the drain that ran under the road. Water from the recent rain was knee-deep and difficult to walk through. They sloshed their way to the middle of the long tunnel. Vicki couldn't see a thing until the car passed above them. The light shone on the right side of the drain, and Vicki saw the silhouette of her two friends beside her.

"Please, God," Vicki whispered, "let him pass."

The light switched to the left side of the road where Maggie's car sat under a mound of debris. Vicki's heart sank as she heard a squeal of brakes above them.

FOUR

Meeting C. W.

Vicki held her breath as the light focused on the culvert where they had left the car. She wondered if they had hidden the car well enough.

"What if Phoenix barks?" Charlie whispered.

Vicki shrugged. "Nothing we can do now."

Darrion pointed to the other end of the drain. "We should go out that side and run."

A radio crackled above, and Vicki moved to the other end of the pipe. She guessed it was Deputy Commander Henderson calling for an update. "Have you found anything?"

"Still looking, sir," the Peacekeeper above them said. "Thought I saw something just now, but it was just a broken tailpipe."

"So that's what happened when we went down the embankment," Darrion whispered.

"Keep looking, and let us know if you find anything," Henderson said.

"Yes, sir."

The car slowly pulled forward. Darrion climbed out of the tunnel and checked their car. She waved Vicki and Charlie up, and they pushed the limbs and debris away.

"Guess we did a pretty good job of hiding it," Charlie said.

Phoenix barked wildly, and Darrion opened the back door and petted him. "Good boy. Way to be quiet."

When the GC car was out of sight, Vicki hopped in and turned the key. The engine roared so loud that Vicki turned off the ignition.

"Can't worry about that now," Darrion said. "Let's go."

Natalie watched the countryside roll by, pretending to dial satellite operations.

Finally, Henderson asked for the phone and dialed himself. It rang through and he pulled to the side and asked for an update. "No, there are three cars, all heading south," he said. "Where? . . . Okay, how far would you say the third car is from them?"

When Henderson hung up he got on the

radio. "You've passed them," he said. "Satellite one said there's a car traveling north between you and the roadblock."

"I couldn't have passed them, sir. I've gone over every inch of road."

"Somebody pulled out a moment ago and is driving north at a high rate of speed. It has to be them. They must have hidden in some cornfield and are trying to get by the road-block. Catch them!"

"I'm on it, sir."

The other two cars radioed and said they were turning around as well. Henderson spun gravel as he drove from the roadside. "We've got them now."

Judd was startled by the Peacekeeper and looked for a place to run. He noticed the young man's nameplate read "Donaldson."

"I said, are you okay?"

"Yeah, I was just thinking about some stuff. Is it all right to sit here?"

"Not a problem. Let me guess what you're thinking about. Have something to do with the potentate rising again?"

Judd nodded. "That's part of it."

The Peacekeeper chuckled and sat. "I've wanted to work for the Global Community ever since I heard about His Excellency. Winding up here was a dream come true."

"Where are you from?"

"United North American States. Tallahas-see, Florida, to be exact. The potentate made a point of hiring from every country so people would know this is truly a Global Community. Where are *you* from?"

Judd told him, being careful not to reveal too much. When the Peacekeeper asked where he was staying, Judd said, "Right now a friend and I are with this musician from the States. He's a singer with The Four Horsemen."

The Peacekeeper's mouth dropped open. "Not Z-Van! You're staying with him?"

Judd shrugged. "We kind of helped him out in Israel."

The Peacekeeper slapped Judd on the back. "That's awesome. I heard some teenagers had rescued him, but I didn't believe it. What's he like?"

"Works alone in his room a lot. He can be kind of annoying, especially at two in the morning."

The Peacekeeper stuck out a hand. "Roy Donaldson."

"I'm Judd . . . er . . . Wayne Judson." They shook hands and Judd sighed. He couldn't believe he'd almost given his real name to the Peacekeeper.

"I suppose you'll stay here and take the mark of loyalty in New Babylon," Donaldson said. "A lot of people are doing that. What kind of identifier are you going to get, Wayne?"

"I . . . uh . . . haven't been able to make up my mind. What about you?"

"I'm going for the big one, you know, the one that covers the whole left side of the forehead. I want to really show them how loyal I am."

"That'll do it," Judd said. "They'll be able to see that a block away."

Judd waited for a chance to talk with Roy about the truth, but the more they talked, the more it became clear that Roy had chosen the wrong path. Unless something happened to lift Carpathia's trance over him, the boy would take the mark and his eternal destiny would be sealed.

Roy stood to leave. "I have to say, I envy you, Wayne. To be in the same hotel room with a star like Z-Van and listen to the songs he's writing about the potentate must be something." He edged closer and handed Judd a piece of paper. "Do you think you might be able to get me an autograph?"

Judd asked Roy to write his name and

address on the paper and said he would have Z-Van send him something.

"Awesome!" Roy said.

When Roy was gone, Judd sat back and ran a hand through his hair. He was about to stand when he heard a rustling behind him. He turned to see a teenage boy in some bushes. He was shorter than Judd, dark hair, clearly Asian. On his forehead was the mark of the believer. He put out his hand. "Are you Judd Thompson?"

"Are you C. W.?"

The boy smiled. "Chang Wong. It's nice to meet you."

Mark held the map in the front seat of Colin Dial's van and watched for the shortcut to Route 12. As soon as Vicki's phone had gone dead, Mark awakened the other kids and asked them to pray. He and Colin had set out immediately for the roadblock, not knowing how much Vicki heard of their instructions.

"If they're following Vicki's car with the satellite, we have another problem," Colin said. "They'll follow our van too."

"Is there any way to block it?"

"If you can come up with some kind of

energy shield before we get there," Colin said, smiling. "If not, our only hope is that God strikes them blind or some clouds roll in."

They passed a small lake and Colin slowed. He turned left onto a dirt road that led past more farmland. "This comes out just inside the old Illinois state line. Let's hope we're in time."

Looking at the road, Vicki knew it would be impossible to drive back up the embankment. But a few yards farther was a more gradual hill. Vicki backed out, the car screeching against a fence by the road, and roared onto the highway. Without the tailpipe, the car sounded like a tank, but it didn't seem to bother anyone but Phoenix.

Vicki hated not having contact with anyone in the Young Trib Force, but with Maggie's cell phone dead and no other means of communication, they were on their own.

The road narrowed to a stretch of rebuilt road. The blacktop was smooth, and the yellow lines in the center seemed to glow in the moonlight. The car crested a small hill and Darrion pointed at a road sign. They were two miles from Wisconsin and probably even closer to the roadblock. Vicki stopped in the middle of the road and rolled down her window.

"What now?" Darrion said.

"Let's get a little closer and look for a place to ditch the car. We can walk into one of those fields and find Mark on the other side."

Darrion frowned. "If he's really on the other side."

"He'll be there," Vicki said.

Darrion scooted closer and covered her mouth with a hand. "We've got another problem. How are we going to get bowser back there to keep quiet while we're tiptoeing through the countryside?"

"You want to leave him?"

"No way," Charlie said from the back. "I know what you're talking about, and we're not leaving Phoenix."

Vicki smiled. "You think you can keep him quiet?"

"I know I can," Charlie said.

Darrion held up a hand and looked behind them. "You hear that?"

"What?" Vicki said, sticking her head out the window.

A whirring sound rose above the noise of the crickets and frogs and the car. Vicki caught the flash of headlights coming over a hill. She glanced in the rearview mirror. A second set of headlights crested a hill behind her.

Phoenix whimpered, and Charlie cradled him in his lap as the car sped down the hill. One half mile later they came to another hill. Vicki noticed something shining at the bottom of the incline. "Quick, everybody out!"

Darrion gathered their things and Charlie picked up Phoenix. Vicki put the car in neutral and wedged a stick against the accelerator, revving the engine.

"What are you doing?" Darrion said.

"Run!" Vicki said as she jammed the car into drive and jumped out of the way.

Tires screeched as the car picked up speed. Vicki watched it cross the center line into the next lane. The roadway dipped, causing the car to swerve right. Just before the bridge, it veered toward an embankment.

Vicki ran into the nearby field and joined Darrion and Charlie. They heard a terrific crash in the distance and rushed into the night.

Natalie craned her neck to see the flashing lights of two GC cruisers ahead. Henderson pulled up to the bridge. Natalie followed him and the other Peacekeeper down the embankment on foot. Maggie's car had smashed against a tree and both doors had

flown open. The air bags had deployed.
Natalie imagined Vicki and the others lying
dead alongside the car.

"Happened a few minutes ago," a Peacekeeper near the car said.

"Anybody in it?" Henderson shouted.

"No. And there doesn't appear to be any
blood around."

Henderson inspected the debris, then
leaned into the car. "It's in neutral. They
must have let it roll from up there." He
turned to Natalie and handed her the cell
phone. "Get satellite on the line now. We
need to know which way they went."

Natalie took the phone, dialed the
number, and asked for the satellite operator
Henderson had been working with. She had
helped the kids escape, but now, by
pinpointing their location on the ground,
she was helping capture them again.

Henderson took the phone. "Yeah, we've
found their car but the kids are gone. Can
you locate anyone on foot? . . . What? That
can't be!" Henderson looked up. "I can see
the moon as clear as day!" He gave the coordinates again. "I don't believe this. All right,
I'm going to stay on the line and let me
know when you make contact."

"What's wrong?" Natalie said.

"New guy took over. He says there's some

interference, but it can't be the clouds. Must be a glitch in the system." Henderson gathered the other Peacekeepers. "You three go west along this creek bank. The three of us will go east. Radio me the second you spot anything."

Vicki ran as quickly and quietly as she could through the tall grass, leading Darrion and Charlie away from the road, then north. Three cars had passed on the road and stopped near the bridge, so she was sure they had found Maggie's car. Would the GC come looking for them away from the road or stay with their cars?

Vicki was exhausted, and she could tell that Darrion and Charlie were tired and scared. Phoenix whimpered and Charlie clamped his mouth shut.

As they neared the creek, the three knelt by the stream. There was movement near the road, but Vicki couldn't see how far away the GC were.

Phoenix suddenly put his paws on the ground and wriggled free. Charlie lunged, but the dog was gone, scampering along the creek toward the road. Darrion grabbed Charlie's arm when he started after the dog.

"I'm sorry, I—"

"Shh," Vicki said. "Let's just get away from here."

"But what about—?"

"Phoenix will take care of himself," Vicki said. "Come on."

Natalie saw Phoenix first. He was coming from the east, trotting along, sniffing at the creek bank.

"Look!" Natalie shouted. "That's the dog!"

Phoenix barked and Henderson unholstered his gun.

"I saw him just loop around us," Natalie continued. "It looked like he came from back toward the road."

"Our cars!" Henderson said. He looked at Natalie. "Get that dog and meet us at the road."

Natalie ran after Phoenix, but the dog dodged her and followed Henderson. She looked into the darkness and prayed for her friends.

Vicki's legs ached as she ran up a knoll and through a cluster of trees. She was sure the satellite would locate them. She stopped and heard a radio crackle from their left, so the kids ran east a few hundred yards, then north.

"I see a road," Darrion whispered a few minutes later.

They ran beside the road until Darrion held up a hand. "I'm turned around. We could be running right toward them."

Two headlights blinded them as a huge vehicle pulled out of the brush. It skidded to a stop in the gravel and a door opened.

"Need a ride?" Mark said.

FIVE

Chang's Dilemma

JUDD shook hands with his new friend, Chang Wong, and Chang suggested they move to a gazebo that was more private. As they walked, Chang talked about the Peacekeeper Donaldson.

"I feel bad for the guy," Judd said. "He seemed so blind."

"From what my sister says, there aren't many Global Community workers left who are open to the truth."

"What does your sister do?"

"Her name is Ming. She has been working at a women's facility in Belgium. The Global Community sent her on assignment here last week."

"She's older than you?"

"Yes, she is twenty-two. Do you have family left?"

Judd shook his head and told Chang the story of his family's disappearance.

"As difficult as it must be to lose your parents and a brother and sister, I wish your story were mine. My mother and father do not know God personally. My father is a devoted follower of Nicolae Carpathia, and I'm afraid of what will happen if my parents find out my sister and I are both believers."

"How did you and your sister discover the truth?"

Chang smiled. "We grew up in China and didn't have much religious training. I studied computers and electronics and different languages."

"Your English is perfect."

"I had a good teacher. Anyway, my sister's story is tragic. She was married two months when the disappearances occurred. Her husband was riding a commuter train that crashed when some of the men controlling it vanished. A short while after Carpathia signed the peace treaty protecting Israel, she joined the Global Community and was assigned to what used to be the Philippines.

"At the same time, I was watching the world fall apart from home. When school resumed, many in my high school were gone. There were rumors that they had been involved in the underground church that had become so big in my country."

"Did you figure it out on your own?"

"I tried to watch Dr. Ben-Judah on television, but my father turned it off. That made me more curious.

"Some friends stumbled onto a meeting place of one of the former underground churches. One whole family that owned a restaurant in our area had disappeared. These boys decided to investigate.

"At the rear of the kitchen they found a false wall. Behind it was a room that would hold as many as one hundred people. Tucked away in a secret compartment were hand-copied Bibles and song sheets. We also found a schedule of meetings. These believers came at all hours of the day and night, one hundred at a time, to pray and study God's Word."

"Incredible," Judd said.

"Yes. Each week hundreds passed through that room and learned the truth of the Bible. Even more incredible is the letter my friends discovered. An envelope was tacked on the wall next to the secret opening. On the outside it read 'If we disappear.' It was as if they knew what was going to happen."

Judd rubbed his arms and felt a chill. He thought about Pastor Bruce Barnes and the video he had found explaining the Rapture. The letter from these Chinese Christians wasn't as high-tech, but it contained the same message.

"What did the letter say?" Judd said.

"I'll show you a copy sometime. Basically it said that if people had disappeared and no one knew where they were, it was because Jesus had come back for his followers. The Rapture happened during the day in China, so many people were injured and even killed because of absent drivers and accidents. The father of my friend Chu Ling was washing windows on a tall building with a man who had talked to him about God for many months. Chu's father looked away for a moment, and when he turned around, the other man was gone. Only his clothes and his squeegee remained."

"What did your friends think of the letter?"

"Some believed right away and prayed the prayer the pastor had written. Chu prayed that day and came to my house immediately. He took me upstairs and locked the door because he was afraid of my father. I read the pastor's letter and it all made sense. For things in the Bible to come true like that was too much of a coincidence.

"Of course, I downloaded a Bible from the Internet almost immediately and started studying and reading Dr. Ben-Judah's Web site. That's when I started writing Ming."

"How did she react?"

"At first, I could tell she didn't want to listen, but we had been good friends through the years and I made her promise that no matter what she decided, she would not tell Mother and Father. I reprinted the letter the pastor had written and included the prayer. I also copied verses from the Bible and sent them to her. Ming finally wrote that she had become a follower of Jesus. It was one of the happiest days of my life."

"And she stayed in the Global Community?"

Chang nodded. "She has tried to help fellow believers."

Chang asked to hear more about the Young Tribulation Force and hung on Judd's every word, from news of the underground newspaper in their high school to the recent satellite transmission from the kids in Illinois.

"You know this Vicki B.?" Chang said.

Judd smiled. "She's one of my best friends. Did you see her?"

"My father required me to go to the meeting. When the Vicki B. segment came on, I noticed her mark and prayed she would be able to continue. The authorities at our site were able to shut off the satellite feed, but only after many had heard and believed the message."

Judd checked his watch. "I should get in touch with my friends and tell them I'm okay."

"Call from my apartment," Chang said.

As they walked, Judd showed Chang the buildings he had visited during his previous trip to New Babylon. He briefly told Chang of Pavel and Pavel's father, Nada, and her brother, Kasim. Chang showed an identification card at the front door, and the guard let them inside.

"So your dad's pushing you to do the same as your sister?"

Chang nodded as they entered a glass elevator and pushed the button to the fourth floor. The Wongs' apartment was number 4054. Chang's mother was small with dark hair and didn't speak English as well as Chang, but Judd understood her enough to carry on a polite conversation. Judd called Lionel and told him what had happened and said he would be back in an hour or two.

"No, you have dinner with us," Mrs. Wong said.

"I really shouldn't—"

"I insist. You meet husband too."

Judd looked at Chang, who shrugged and

cocked his head. "Looks like you're staying for dinner."

Chang took Judd to his room. "We have to be careful, especially during dinner. My father will ask you many questions about your allegiance to the potentate and what you plan to do in service to the GC."

"I understand. Now tell me what's going on."

"I know I might help the cause if I work for the GC," Chang said, "but we already have someone inside the communications center. Plus, I'm not sure I can stomach being close to Carpathia. The things I saw at the resurrection nearly made me want to jump up and shout my trust in God."

"Where were you sitting?"

"In the VIP area near the main stage. When Fortunato called down fire on the three rebel potentates, we were so close I could smell the smoke. My father was in tears when Nicolae pushed that Plexiglas coffin lid off and stood up. I don't even want to think about that day. A lot of believers were killed by the lightning."

"So why can't you just tell your dad the truth? He'd understand, wouldn't he?"

"You don't know my father," Chang said. "The other reason I can't work for the Global

Community is Carpathia's mark. All employees are required to receive the biochip injection and the mark within a few weeks, but I have heard rumors that new hires will be first in line."

Judd nodded. "Makes sense. That way they hire you knowing you're loyal."

"Exactly. And I will die before I take Carpathia's mark."

"If you told your dad that, he'd never make you work for the guy."

"If I admit I am a follower of Christ and an enemy of Nicolae, Father will report me. That's how loyal he is to the potentate. But it's not only my life that's at stake. I am afraid he will demand to know the truth about Ming."

"What does she say about all this?"

"She thinks I should remain quiet, but I don't know how I can."

"Come with us," Judd said. "The Young Trib Force will hide you."

Chang smiled. "Thank you. I've thought about that. I'm afraid the GC would catch me and that would kill my father."

The front door opened, and a man spoke loudly in the next room. "That's him," Chang said as he led Judd to the kitchen area. The man's English was slightly better than his wife's, and he spoke rapidly and forcefully.

Judd noticed Chang's shoulders droop when his father talked.

"I visit Personnel Department today. Show your grades, letters of recommendation, whole thing. They like it and say they will take your information straight to top. What do you think?"

Mr. Wong slapped Chang on the back and beamed. Chang grabbed Judd's shoulder and pulled him forward. "I'd like you to meet my new friend from the former United States."

"United North American States now," Mr. Wong said. He eyed Judd and thrust out his hand. "You applying to work with Global Community too?"

Judd smiled and nearly laughed, but he composed himself, crossing his arms over his chest. "Uh, no sir, I'm just visiting."

"He's staying with Z-Van, the famous singer," Chang said.

Mr. Wong nodded. "Much talent. Very loyal to His Excellency. Music too loud, but I can plug my ears."

"Dinner in one hour," Mrs. Wong said, and Chang led Judd back to his room.

Vicki kept looking behind the van, sure that the GC would find them using the satellite.

Mark filled her in on what had happened to the kids since they had separated. She couldn't believe the danger the kids had encountered or the way God had moved among the people at the shelter.

When Mark pulled the van into the parking area of the underground hideout in Wisconsin, Vicki finally felt safe. She couldn't wait to see the others. Shelly was the first to hug her, and Janie brought food for them.

"I'm too tired to eat," Vicki said.

The others wouldn't let her go until they had heard what had happened in Des Plaines. Darrion helped tell the story. When they finished, Conrad opened the van door and looked around. "Where's Phoenix?"

Vicki explained what had happened. Charlie apologized and everyone assured him it wasn't his fault. The kids asked about the Shairtons' farm, but Charlie was too emotional to talk. "I'll tell you in the morning."

"I think we ought to pray and thank God," Shelly said after Vicki had finished her story.

The kids joined hands and thanked God for keeping them safe and providing food and shelter. After a few minutes, Charlie said, "And, God, I want to thank you for giving me friends that would risk their lives for me. And I ask you to take care of Bo and Ginny in that jail. Help them get out of there. And for Mr. Zeke too. Be with them every step of the way."

"And for Maggie and Natalie," Vicki prayed. "Help them to not get in trouble for helping us."

"And Phoenix," Janie said. "I know he's just a dog, but he's been a big part of this group from the start. Protect him and bring him back to us."

Shelly showed Vicki to a shower, and a few minutes later Vicki crawled into bed between fresh sheets.

As the sun came up on the Wisconsin hideout, Vicki was twenty feet underground in darkness, dreaming of her friend Ryan Daley. He was laughing and playing with Phoenix, just like the day they had first met.

SIX

The Dinner

JUDD prayed with Chang about the GC job and his parents. He asked God to give Chang clear direction. Chang prayed for Judd, Lionel, and their new friend Westin.

Mrs. Wong called them to dinner. When everyone was seated, Mr. Wong folded his hands and closed his eyes. He said a few words in Chinese, then began eating.

Chang glanced at Judd. "My father just gave thanks to Carpathia for the apartment and the food."

Mr. Wong slammed down his fork and scowled. "You not call him that. You say His Excellency or Lord Carpathia. Never use only last name, understand?"

"Yes, Father."

Mrs. Wong passed Judd a full plate. He tried to avoid eye contact with Mr. Wong, but the man kept looking at him.

"How you meet my son?"

Judd carefully wiped his mouth with a napkin, thinking quickly how much information he wanted to share. "We were on a Web site a bunch of friends and I put together."

Chang kicked Judd under the table.

"What Web site?"

"It's harmless, really. We talk about things going on in the world and try to figure out what will happen next."

"What you think of Carpathia coming back to life?"

Judd took a mouthful of food and sat back. He swallowed and leaned forward. "We actually nailed that one."

Mr. Wong frowned. "Nailed? What is nailed?"

"They predicted it before it happened," Chang said. "Father, why do you have to interrogate my friends?"

"I ask question. What so wrong with that?"

"I don't mind," Judd said.

Chang's mother said something in Chinese that angered Mr. Wong. The two sat in silence. Finally, Mr. Wong started a conversation about the new Nicolae. "I hear today that potentate not need sleep. He stay up twenty-four hours every day."

Judd knew this was because Carpathia was inhabited by Satan. Judd didn't want to think of all the wicked things Nicolae had prepared for the world. He knew the man would eventually rise up against Jewish people and believers, but most would blindly follow him.

"You say you not here to work for Global Community," Mr. Wong said. "Why you here?"

Judd didn't want to lie to the man. Mr. Wong needed to know God just like everyone else. But if he was loyal enough to pray to Carpathia, he was surely under the spell of the evil one.

"I'm actually here against my will," Judd said.

Mr. Wong frowned. "You kidnapped?"

"Not exactly." Judd told the story of finding Z-Van in the rubble of the earthquake in Israel and how they had been promised a flight home. "We changed course and headed for New Babylon. Z-Van wanted to attend the funeral and that's why I'm here."

"You see the man rise from the dead in person?"

Judd nodded.

"Most incredible thing ever."

Judd kept nodding. "I can't think of the right words to describe it."

Mr. Wong looked at Chang and said something in Chinese. "Very soon I have two children working for Global Community. Our daughter, Ming, she is Peacekeeper."

"Chang told me you were all together during the . . . funeral service."

"What a day. And soon my own son work for most wonderful leader world has ever seen."

"Father, I haven't even graduated high school."

"So? You could teach high school. They have tutors here. I talk with leader few minute ago. Very high up in Global Community. He say they want you."

"For what? You know they're not going to—"

"He say they let you complete school here."

"But what department would take a—"

Mr. Wong smacked the table. "You genius! No question. You program any computer, fix any electronic in house. You the future of Global Community."

Chang rolled his eyes. "If I'm the future, the Global Community is in big trouble."

"No!" Mrs. Wong said. "Husband right. After paperwork through, you work for Mr. Fortunato—"

"Supreme Commander!" Mr. Wong yelled.

"Yes, sorry," Mrs. Wong said.

Chang dropped his fork noisily. "What paperwork?" A pause as Mr. Wong eyed his son. "Father, what have you done?"

"I give documents to Personnel Department. Application and transcripts already through."

Chang rose and pushed his chair back from the table. "You had no right to do that. I told you I can't work for them. Stop pushing me!"

"You get used to being away from your mother and—"

"That's not it!" Chang yelled. "I'm not working for the GC, and that's final."

Chang stomped from the room and slammed his door. Mr. Wong shook his head and kept eating. Judd looked at his food and tried to think of a way out of the apartment.

Mr. Wong leaned toward Judd and smiled. "He afraid to leave home, but this an opportunity of lifetime."

"Maybe it's more than being away from you. Maybe he's not GC material."

"He perfect GC material. He change mind when he find out about mark."

"What do you mean?"

"You promise not to tell?" Mr. Wong looked toward Chang's door and chuckled. "Man on phone is named Akbar. Big in Global Community government. He say Chang's résumé already get to His Excellency. Potentate actually talk about Chang." Mr. Wong rubbed his hands together with delight. "Only a matter of time before he is processed. Then he sign more papers, the Global Community make offer, and Chang take mark of loyalty."

"But if Chang doesn't want to—"

"It settled. Chang will be among first to take mark, and I be there to watch."

Judd's heart sank. He knew Chang would die before he took the mark of Carpathia. He excused himself from the table and headed toward Chang's bedroom.

Mr. Wong stood. "You go now. Chang upset. We leave him alone."

Judd nodded. "Okay, maybe I'll call him later tonight."

"Not good idea. You go."

Judd thanked Mrs. Wong for dinner, and Mr. Wong walked him to the elevator. Judd asked if he would have any trouble getting out of the building, and Mr. Wong shook his head and stared at Judd.

"I have bad feeling about you."

"I don't understand," Judd said.

"All through dinner you never talk about Potentate. Not say anything good or bad, except that you predict his coming back to life."

"What do you want me to say?"

The elevator dinged and the door opened. A young couple in Peacekeeper uniforms stood at the back. Mr. Wong bowed to them slightly and ushered Judd into the car. "You no call my son."

As Judd walked to the hotel, he tried to think of a plan to get Chang out of New Babylon. No matter what, he had to do it before the GC tried to give him Carpathia's mark.

Vicki awakened in a darkened room and couldn't remember where she was. A clock by the bed glowed 2:17, but since there were no windows she couldn't tell whether it was morning or afternoon. She lay back, closed her eyes, and thought of Natalie and Maggie. She wondered if Deputy Commander Henderson had pieced the plot together.

A mechanical whir sounded through the air ducts overhead. She heard muffled conversation through the vents and recognized Charlie's voice.

When Vicki emerged from the small bedroom, Shelly gave her something to eat and ushered her into a living area complete with a television monitor that doubled as a computer screen.

"We were wondering when you'd wake up," Shelly said.

Mark introduced Colin Dial's wife, Becky.

She was tall with blonde hair and Vicki guessed about forty. Becky smiled. "If you need anything, all you have to do is ask."

"I could use a toothbrush," Vicki said.

"Ready for a tour?" Mark said as Becky went to the supply cabinet.

"I need to talk with Charlie first."

Vicki found Charlie with Conrad and Janie. Charlie was clearly sad about losing Phoenix, and the others tried to console him.

When he saw her, Charlie stood and hugged Vicki. "I didn't get to tell you last night how glad I was to see you. You and Darrion risked your lives for me."

"Nothing you wouldn't have done for us."

They all sat as Charlie began his story. "After you guys left Bo and Ginny's farm, we settled in. I was so worried about you guys the first night I couldn't sleep. Then we read the e-mail that said you'd made it and I felt better.

"These GC guys came back a couple of days later. They had found the satellite truck where you guys hid it and wanted to ask Bo more questions. The guy said he knew the satellite truck had been in the barn."

"He must have noticed that first day," Mark said. "Why didn't you get out of there?"

"We thought everything was going to be okay. Bo said they'd leave us alone, but they didn't. We heard clicks on the phone line, and Ginny said they were listening." Charlie stared off, thinking.

"What is it?" Vicki said.

"Remember when I asked you if we were going to die before Jesus came back?"

Vicki nodded, recalling their long talk the night the kids left for Wisconsin.

"Well, you said a lot of believers were going to be killed in the next couple of years. When the GC came for us, all I could think of was whether we would be some of the first to die, and it scared me."

Mark put a hand on Charlie's shoulder. "I don't blame you. It scares me just to hear your story."

"What happened the night I called?" Vicki said.

"Bo saw some GC cars from the barn loft, so he knew they were watching us. He pulled his car to the back of the house, and we loaded up a bunch of stuff."

"Why didn't you e-mail us?" Vicki said. "We would have helped."

"I told Ginny it would be okay, but she wanted to be careful."

"That was smart," Mark said.

"Bo and Ginny fought about what to do. She wanted to just drive away right then, but

Bo said we should wait and leave after dark. We were going to drive through one of the fields to get to the road."

"But they came for you," Vicki said.

Charlie nodded. "We turned all the lights off so they'd think we were asleep. Ginny wrapped some of her stuff in a blanket so it wouldn't break and took down all her picture albums. That's when she freaked."

"Why?" Vicki said.

"One of her big albums was missing. Bo said they were only three and a half years from seeing Jesus and not to get upset over a bunch of faded pictures, but she got really mad. She said if the GC had that album there wouldn't be any pictures of me. They'd know I wasn't their son."

"So that's how they pieced it together," Mark said.

"Ginny took the rest of her stuff to the car and came running back inside. Said somebody was moving around outside."

"Creepy," Janie said.

"We locked the doors, and I helped Bo move some stuff to block the front door. Then we went into the cellar. We could hear radios outside and Bo said just to keep quiet. That's when you called, Vicki."

"If I'd known you were in that much trouble, I wouldn't have called."

"They started banging on the doors, trying to get inside. Ginny told me not to talk, so I put the phone down. That's when they crashed through the windows. We could hear them walking around upstairs, so we kept quiet. For a while we thought we were going to be okay, but then something bumped the cellar door and stuff started dripping through the boards."

"Gasoline," Mark said.

Charlie nodded. "Bo and I flew up the stairs and tried to open the cellar, but they had it blocked."

"I can't believe they tried to burn you alive," Janie said.

"They use fire against believers everywhere," Mark said.

"How did you get out of the cellar?" Vicki said.

"I told Bo to move and I kicked the door-knob off. It took about three good hits to get it open, but I finally did it. The fire started at the back of the house." Charlie's lip quivered. "I really thought we were going to die."

Vicki closed her eyes and imagined the fire spreading through the farmhouse. Everything the Shairtons owned was gone in minutes.

Charlie held up his left arm, and Vicki noticed a five-inch-long gash. "I helped

Ginny through the window and got this. Bo's clothes caught on fire and we had to roll him on the ground, but he was okay."

"And they took you into custody?" Mark said.

"They weren't real happy we made it out, but they put us in different cars and brought us all the way back to Des Plaines. The guy in the front kept asking if I knew where Ben-Judah was, and I told him I didn't have any idea."

"I'm glad we got you out of there," Vicki said.

"Me too," Charlie said. "But I keep thinking about Ginny and Bo. If we don't get them out, they'll die."

SEVEN

The Cellblock

NATALIE sat at a desk near Deputy Commander Henderson's office with a blank yellow legal pad before her. She listened to the talk around the office, the whispers at the watercooler, the hushed conversation behind partially closed office doors that Henderson might be reassigned.

Natalie had spent the hours after the chase in Wisconsin in fear for her life, wondering if Henderson would piece together the facts and blame her. But a strange turn of events caused Henderson and his companions to trust her again.

After searching for Vicki and the others until early in the morning, Henderson had left the area and driven to Maggie Carlson's home in Des Plaines. Natalie rode along, apologizing for her part in letting the kids get away. Henderson didn't say much, clearly upset that they weren't able to track the kids by satellite.

At Maggie's house, things quickly fell apart. Henderson accused the woman of giving false information about her vehicle to throw them off. Maggie listened quietly and ran her hand across the tablecloth. "I knew you'd figure it out sooner or later," she said. "I helped those girls escape and I'm glad I did."

"You're one of them, aren't you?" Henderson scowled.

"I serve the true, risen Savior, Jesus Christ," Maggie said. "I'll do anything to give that message. I'll protect anyone who is a fellow believer. Helping those kids escape is one of the best things I've done in my life."

"It will be one of the last things you do," Henderson said as he handcuffed the woman and led her to the car.

After arriving at the jail and helping process the woman, Natalie walked back to her apartment, wondering about Maggie's future and why the satellite hadn't worked the night before. Had God blinded the operators somehow?

The next day Natalie sat at her desk and filled out forms explaining her story, but something still wasn't right. She phoned the satellite operations number, and a woman flipped through the logbook. "Looks like Brad was on until late. Then Jim Dekker relieved him."

Natalie explained why she was calling, and the woman reluctantly gave Dekker's home phone number. Natalie called and left a message.

She scribbled on the yellow legal pad, feeling alone. This was one way of talking to someone, even if it was only a sheet of paper staring at her.

1. *Leave and find V. and others.*
2. *Stay and keep out of Henderson's way.*
3. *Stay and help Maggie, Ginny, Bo, and Zeke.*

The first option seemed the safest. She could simply contact Vicki, find a ride north, and meet up with the Young Tribulation Force in Wisconsin. She crossed out option 1.

The second option was a good one. Natalie could do her job, blend into the surroundings, and keep the Young Trib Force alerted to the GC's movements. If a new leader came in, which was almost sure to happen, she could make herself almost invisible.

She crossed out option 2 and studied option 3. *If I don't try to help, I'll never forgive myself,* Natalie thought.

She tore the page off the pad and shredded it in a nearby machine. Something blipped on the computer in Henderson's office and Natalie pulled up the network e-mail. A system-wide message marked "urgent" had just been sent by GC headquarters to "all United North American States personnel."

All jails, prisons, and reeducation centers will receive shipment of the first loyalty enforcement facilitators within seven to ten days.

Why don't they just call them neck and head separators? Natalie thought.

The biochip injectors will ship separately directly from New Babylon. All Global Community personnel should refer to the machines with the exact terminology used above. The loyalty enforcement facilitators should not be called guillotines, and their use will not be referred to as a beheading. We will not use language that causes the public to think of violence or causes followers to think we are forcing people against their will.

Natalie sighed. *So we shouldn't say, "Take Carpathia's mark or we'll chop off your head!"*

On the contrary, the Global Community has been forced to implement this needed equipment to maintain peace and harmony for the people of the world. In fact, we hope we never need the loyalty enforcement facilitators and believe only a few enemies who see themselves as martyrs will even consider not taking the mark of loyalty.

The message listed sites around the country and added that the first United North American States location to apply the mark would be the former DuPage County Jail in Illinois. Natalie checked a calendar. She had to save her friends or they would prove the Global Community wrong. There were many who wouldn't take Carpathia's mark, and she was one of them.

Judd met with Lionel and Westin about Chang's situation. They agreed the only safe plan was to get Chang away from his father, which meant having him hide or even return with Judd and Lionel to the States.

"How about Israel?" Lionel said. "He could stay with Mr. Stein."

"I don't think Z-Van's up for more company," Westin said. "He talked about you two this morning and asked what I thought about ditching you."

Judd's mouth dropped open. "What did you say?"

"Didn't say anything. He floats stuff like this a lot just to see how you react. I think he thinks I'm kind of attached to you guys."

"Maybe we shouldn't go to Israel after all," Lionel said.

Westin held up a hand. "Z-Van's kept you around this long. Don't bail yet."

"What about Chang?" Judd said.

"Keep in touch with him. They'll have to give him a date when they want him to start work. We'll get him out before he takes the mark."

Vicki asked Mark to show her around outside the underground shelter. Mark took her through a series of doors that led out. The hideout was well hidden, and Mark explained why Colin had built the shelter.

Vicki looked out on the Wisconsin countryside. "I think I could live here."

Mark took her inside the small house where Colin and Becky lived. "There's another level to the underground. Come on."

Beneath the living area, even farther underground, was storage for food, water, and an emergency generator in case of a power outage. Mark opened another door into a darkened room and Vicki stepped inside.

"You ready for this?" Mark said.

Vicki nodded and Mark turned on the lights. On the length of the back wall was a map of the world with pins placed in various cities. Around the room were different types of computers and printers, most of them turned off. There were three smaller rooms to the side with recording equipment, cameras, and other high-tech gear.

"What's all this for?" Vicki said.

"Colin and his wife were just going to use this as living space, but he really wanted to use this place to reach more people. They have a friend who's a computer whiz, and he found a lot of this at churches and Christian ministries. The rest of it Colin bought."

"What's the map for?"

"The red pins are GC outposts," Mark said, pointing at Des Plaines. "If there's a yellow pin, it means he knows there's somebody on the inside who's a believer."

Vicki saw at least fifty yellow pins in North America alone. "But what's all this for?"

Mark shrugged. "Colin doesn't know yet."

"Do you think it has something to do with us?"

Mark sat at one of the working computers and pulled up the kids' Web site. "If we could get everybody working on something, pulling together all these resources, there's no telling what we could do. We could hack into GC mainframes with the right passwords and change information. We could send e-mails, help Chloe Williams's co-op, communicate with all of these believers at the different GC sites—"

"You have to remember that they won't be working there much longer. Once they make them take Carpathia's mark they'll have to run or die."

Mark turned to the computer and pulled up a drawing. "This is a mock-up of Carpathia's mark. Colin's friend figured out a way to make it into a fake tattoo."

"And fool the GC?"

"Right. We hack into the GC records and make them think the believers already have the mark. Of course, we have to find out if it looks enough like the real thing, but it could be done."

Vicki sat and stared at the floor. She thought of Bo, Ginny, Zeke, and Maggie. *What about them?* She thanked God for bringing them to Colin and Becky's place.

"And please," she prayed silently, "show us what to do next."

When Natalie saw her chance, she grabbed a file folder from a stack near Deputy Commander Henderson's office and went downstairs to the holding area. Women's cells were on the north side of the building, and the men were on the south.

Natalie showed her identification and looked in the folder. "Just a couple of questions Henderson wants answered of the Judah-ite."

The guard nodded and buzzed the door. Natalie walked through confidently and heard the lock click behind her. She passed several women sleeping in the dimly lit cellblock and heard someone whispering down the corridor. Maggie Carlson was talking with a woman in the cell next to her. Maggie glanced at Natalie and winked. Natalie walked to the end of the row and heard verses of an old hymn. "Are you Ginny?"

The woman glanced at the mark on Natalie's forehead and nodded. "When I was little, I learned a lot of songs at a country church. I thought they were old-fashioned at the time, but the words stuck with me."

"It sounds beautiful."

Ginny took Natalie's hand. "Do you know anything about my husband?"

Natalie shook her head. "I haven't been in the men's side and don't know if they'll let me in, but I came to tell you that Charlie is safe."

Ginny put a hand to her mouth and whispered, "Praise God."

Natalie briefly told her what had happened and that Vicki and Darrion were safe too. "I'm trying to get you and your husband out of here before they start giving people the mark."

Ginny shook her head. "It's too dangerous."

Natalie's lip quivered. "If you stay here, they're going to make you take Carpathia's mark, and the only option—"

The door opened at the end of the hall, and the female guard yelled, "You okay?"

"Yeah, almost through."

When the door closed, Ginny reached through the cell bars, took Natalie by the shoulders, and locked eyes with the girl. "Listen to me. It does my heart good to know Charlie and the others are safe. You risked your life to do that, and I'm sure you wouldn't hesitate to risk it again for us. But you have to understand that we're ready to go."

"What do you mean?"

"I've had one thing on my prayer list since

I became a believer, and that's my husband, Bo. Charlie and the others told him the truth and somehow God opened his eyes. I'm forever grateful for that."

"But you don't understand. They're going to kill you if—"

"I do understand. Bo and I talked about what we'd do if the GC caught us and made us swear loyalty to Carpathia. I don't look forward to it, but from what Dr. Ben-Judah wrote, we know God will give us the strength we need at just the right time."

Natalie wiped away a tear. "I'm still going to try."

Ginny smiled and slipped a piece of paper in the girl's hand. "If you can, pass this along to my husband. And don't blame yourself if you can't get us out of here. Just make sure you're safe."

Natalie nodded and slowly turned down the hallway. Behind her came the words, "He is risen!"

She turned, looked back at Ginny, and with tears in her eyes repeated the words meant not for Carpathia, but for Jesus Christ. "He is risen indeed!"

EIGHT

Fearless Zeke

NATALIE wiped away a tear and straightened her uniform. She held her cell phone to her ear and waved at the guard through a small window.

"That's what the woman told me," she said as the guard opened the door. "You want me to talk with the husband?"

The guard sat at a small desk, leafing through a magazine. Natalie put her hand over the mouthpiece and said, "The deputy commander wants me to speak with the husband."

The guard looked up and winced. "We don't usually allow females—"

"You want to talk with my boss?" Natalie said, holding out the phone.

"No, that's okay. If he wants you in there, go ahead."

While the women's side had seemed subdued, the men's side was noisy. The guard walked a few feet inside the cellblock. "Stay in the middle, miss."

Natalie slowly walked down the corridor. She had heard of the arrest of several gang members only days before, and as she walked, she sensed the eyes of the inmates on her.

An older man spoke over the hoots of other prisoners. Some yelled for him to shut up while others wanted to hear him.

"You think you know the truth and the rest of us are idiots!" one prisoner said.

"Yeah, old man, what makes you an expert on religion?" another said. "Owning a gas station?"

Some laughed and made jokes about pumping gas for God, but the older man wouldn't quit. "I never said I was an expert, but you don't have to have a degree to see what's happening. Everything that's going on in the world was predicted in the Bible thousands of years ago. Pretty soon, they're going to come in here and lead us out one by one and tell us we have to take Carpathia's mark. I'm warning you, if you take that mark, your eternal destiny will be sealed."

"What happens if we don't take it?" a man yelled.

"They'll kill you."

Several men groaned loudly. One said, "I'll take my chances with the mark. I don't want to die."

A thin man behind Natalie called out, "Carpathia's a monster. I don't trust somebody who kills people who disagree with him. I won't take the mark either."

"But it won't do any good to refuse the mark without receiving the forgiveness God offers," the older man said. "Accept it now, before it's too late."

"Listen to him!" a man said near Natalie. He had a higher voice and spoke with a slight accent. "My wife tried to tell me the truth for a long time, but I wouldn't listen. It took a kid showing me the Bible to make me believe."

"Are you Bo?" Natalie said.

The man nodded.

Natalie held out the piece of paper. "It's from your wife."

Bo took the paper and thanked Natalie, recognizing the mark of the believer on her forehead. "What are you doing in here, sister?"

"I wanted to talk with you and Zeke about getting out of here," Natalie whispered.

Bo smiled. "I don't think you could get

Zeke out if you tried. He's got a captive audience."

As Natalie approached his cell, Zeke turned to a younger Hispanic man with tattoos on his face, neck, and arms. "You remind me of my son."

"Mister, I don't understand the prophecies you talked about, but I used to hear about God in my mother's church. The priest said Jesus died for each of us, but I never did more than look at him up on that cross."

"What's your name?"

"Manny."

"Manny, Jesus did die on that cross for you. He lived a perfect life, no sin at all. But you've sinned, haven't you?"

Manny lowered his head and nodded. "I've done bad things."

"We all have," Zeke said.

"There is no way he could forgive me."

Zeke stared at the boy. "God loved you so much that he sent his only Son into the world so that anyone who believes in him, or puts his trust in him, won't be separated from God after they die, but they'll have eternal life."

"But you don't know. I would have to spend a lifetime trying to make it up to God."

"Once you sin, you're guilty, no matter how big or how small that sin. You can't go back and change that. That's why Jesus took your place. He lived a perfect life, and God accepted his sacrifice on your behalf. All you have to do is reach out in faith and ask him to come into your life."

The cellblock hushed as Manny sat on his cot. Natalie needed to speak with Zeke, but she waited, standing in the shadows by his cell.

"I have to warn you that if you go through with this, you won't be able to accept Carpathia's mark."

"What do you mean?"

"When you ask God to come into your life and forgive you, he seals you with a mark on your forehead. We can't see it yet, but we will once you've prayed."

A man hurled insults at Zeke and told him he was crazy. Others quieted him as Zeke stared at Manny.

"God won't let you take the evil one's mark because you're his," Zeke continued. "You see, the world is taking sides. Either you're on God's side, or you're on the side of evil. There's no straddling the fence."

"I want to pray," Manny whispered. "I want to be on God's side, no matter what happens."

"All right, then go ahead and tell God you're sorry."

Manny took a deep breath. "God, I'm sorry for killing that guy. And for all the stuff I stole and for the drugs . . ." Manny kept praying, whispering sin after sin until he was finished.

"Now pray with me," Zeke said. "God, I believe you sent your Son to die in my place and that he rose from the dead, and right now I want to accept the gift you're offering me. I ask you to forgive me of all of those sins I've committed, wash me clean, and be my Lord from now on, amen."

Manny prayed along with Zeke and looked up with tears in his eyes. "I feel like I've just had a hundred pounds taken off my back."

A prisoner laughed and others mocked Manny. "God, forgive him for kicking his dog!" one yelled.

Natalie heard a noise and saw a man with a mustache looking through the window at the end of the hall. She glanced away. When she looked back, the man was gone.

Manny stood and wiped his eyes, ignoring the jeers. His face lit up when he saw Zeke's forehead. Then he pointed at Natalie. "She has one too!"

Zeke turned. "Is there something I can help you with?"

"I'm trying to find a way for you to escape," Natalie whispered. "Manny too."

Zeke smiled. "I appreciate you risking your life. But there comes a time when a man has to take a stand."

"I can't let them—"

"You don't understand. I'm a trophy for the GC. They've charged me with selling fuel oil on the black market, but they know I'm a rebel. Anybody who tries to help me will be in the same boat. I've made peace with God. The only thing bothering me now is getting the rest of these guys to see the truth and to find out about my son. I'd like to know he's all right."

Natalie told Zeke about Vicki and the other kids in the Young Tribulation Force and that there had been a fire at the gas station. "The GC never found any bodies, so I'm sure your son made it out."

Zeke bowed his head and shook with emotion. "I've been praying God would send somebody to tell me about him. I know he'd get a message to me if he could, but that would only put him and the people of the Tribulation Force in danger."

The door at the end of the hall opened and the guard stepped inside. Zeke yelled, "Why'd you send a girl down here to do a man's job? I told you I'd never tell you what you want to know!"

The guard quickly walked toward Natalie.

"This might be the last time I get to come here," Natalie whispered.

"Then remember this," Zeke whispered. "Forget about getting me out of here and get yourself to safety. They'll be making you take that mark pretty soon."

"Miss Bishop?" the guard said. "It's time."

Natalie turned and walked away. She glanced at Bo who was sitting on his cot, reading his wife's letter. He mouthed, "Thank you," as she passed. Behind her she heard Zeke say, "He is risen!"

Natalie whispered, "He is risen indeed."

Natalie thanked the guard and told her she hadn't learned as much as she wanted. She sprinted up the back stairway and hurried to her desk. She wanted to quickly e-mail Vicki and the others in Wisconsin but knew she had to wait. Her phone rang and she picked it up.

"This is Jim Dekker of satellite operations. You called my house?"

"Yes, Mr. Dekker, I'm sorry to bother you. I just wanted to ask about the other night."

"Is this from you or Deputy Commander Henderson?"

"Well, he may want to talk again, but I'm curious about the conditions during our chase. When we got out of Des Plaines, it seemed like the sky cleared, so I don't understand—"

"How many times do I have to tell you people? You can look at the record for yourself."

"But how do you explain it? If it's clear from the ground, doesn't that mean you should have been able to see?"

"Unless there was some kind of interference. I can't explain it."

Natalie smiled. "Well, thanks for the information. . . ."

"Before you hang up, I have a couple of questions for you."

"Shoot."

"Is the reason you're asking because you think this whole thing might have been caused by God?"

Natalie forced a laugh. "Why would you think that?"

"Just a hunch. And another thing, what's a Morale Monitor doing in the jail area asking questions of prisoners?"

Natalie looked at the caller ID on the phone. It read "Private." "I don't know what you're talking about."

"I think you do. And if you have the right to ask me questions, I think I deserve some answers."

Natalie didn't know what Jim Dekker was up to, but she felt like slamming down the phone and running out of the building. By the time he could call the GC, perhaps she could be far enough away that they wouldn't catch her. She took a breath. "I was delivering something for my boss."

"Right," Dekker laughed. "Okay, how about this one. Why didn't you handcuff that kid in the backseat? You know, the one who was supposed to have maced you?"

"You want to check my eyes, buddy? They're still red from that stuff."

"I believe it. I also believe you sprayed yourself to make it look like one of them did it."

"Look, if you're going to accuse me of something, you'd better have proof!"

"All right, I accuse you. Ready for the charge?"

"Just say it!"

"Natalie Bishop is a Morale Monitor gone bad. You're a follower of Tsion Ben-Judah. You're employed by the Global Community, but you're really working against it. You have no loyalty to Nicolae Carpathia and you think his rising from the dead proves he's evil. For some reason you're visiting prisoners. Maybe you're trying to help them escape like you helped those kids last night."

Natalie sat down hard, her mouth open. She couldn't speak for a moment.

"You want me to continue?"

"No, I mean . . . that's crazy. Who are you?"

"I told you who I am. Now why don't you tell me who you really are, you Judah-ite."

Natalie looked at the nearest exit. If she grabbed the keys to Deputy Commander Henderson's car, she could be in the parking lot in seconds.

"I'll tell you another thing," Dekker said. "You're wondering how you're going to avoid taking the mark of Carpathia and still work for the GC."

"I have to go," Natalie said.

"Hang on—"

"I'm not talking to you anymore!"

She slammed the phone down and looked around the corner. There was no way to get past Deputy Commander Henderson's secretary without her seeing.

Natalie walked past a row of empty desks and looked for car keys. Nothing. Leaving on foot wasn't the best idea, but she had to get to an exit.

The stairwell door was only a few feet away when an office door on her left opened and a tall man with a mustache stepped out. "Going somewhere, Natalie?"

NINE

Jim Dekker

NATALIE caught her breath and stepped back. She put a hand on her chest and smiled. "You scared me!"

The man wore a flak jacket and dark clothing. He was tall—Natalie guessed over six feet—thin, wore glasses, black boots, and a baseball cap with the letters GCSD. "Didn't mean to frighten you, Natalie. Why don't you step in the office?"

"This is Peacekeeper Vesario's office. What are you—?"

The man grabbed her arm. Natalie wanted to scream but in a flash she was pulled inside, the door closed. She gritted her teeth and rubbed her arm. "Who are you? What do you want with me?"

The man sat on the edge of Vesario's desk and crossed his arms. "I'd like some answers to my questions."

"What are you talking about? I've never met you."

The man took out an identification card from his shirt pocket. It read "Jim Dekker, Global Community Satellite Division."

Natalie finally figured it out. Dekker was the man who had looked inside the cellblock earlier. How long had he been watching her? Did he just suspect she was a Judah-ite or did he have evidence?

"Look, I can explain about going into the jail."

"Can you? How about the part about being a follower of Tsion Ben-Judah?"

Natalie put a hand in her pocket and felt for her key ring.

"I'll bet when you hear the phrase 'He is risen,' you don't think about Nicolae at all." Dekker raised his eyebrows and smiled. "Am I right?"

"You have no proof," Natalie said. "I've been a faithful employee—"

"Until you made a couple of mistakes with those kids. I went back in the files and saw you were at the youth event where the satellite truck was stolen. Care to explain that?"

Natalie slowly twisted the top on the Mace dispenser inside her pocket. This man knew exactly who she was. She had to get out of

Vesario's office, out of the building, and out of the Morale Monitors forever.

Dekker stood and took a few steps toward the door, turning his back to her. Natalie pulled the Mace dispenser from her pocket and aimed.

"The truth is, you don't need to explain anything," Dekker said, slipping his identification card in his pocket. "I'm the one who should explain."

He put a hand to his head and turned. Natalie aimed at the man's eyes but stopped when he took off his hat. On his forehead was the mark of the believer!

Natalie fell to her knees, shaken. "Why did you do that?"

Jim Dekker knelt beside her. "Wanted to see how you'd react to a little pressure. And I came down here to make sure my hunch was right."

"How did you know?"

Dekker shrugged. "That car chase was strange. Seemed like a setup. I found the report and wondered if this Maggie lady was the only believer involved. I spotted your mark when you were in the men's cellblock."

"So the satellite did see everything."

Dekker nodded. "I watched one of the operators handle it. He had those kids nailed. There was no way they were going to get away."

"What did you do?"

"The guy wanted to keep going until we caught them, even though his shift was over. I convinced him to leave, told him I'd make sure everything worked out. He hung around for another fifteen minutes, the longest fifteen minutes of my life. When he was gone, I programmed a glitch, then covered it up so they couldn't find it."

"I thought it was something God did to blind the operators."

"Well, I think God had something to do with it. He put me there, and I wasn't even supposed to be working. Something told me I needed to be there."

Natalie shook her head. God's protection astounded her. "How did I do with the pressure?"

Jim smiled. "Fine. I need you to keep your cool for a few more days. If we're going to get your friends out before they start applying the mark, I'll need you right here."

"How are you—?"

"Trust me." Jim pulled a plastic case from a pocket and gave it to Natalie. "I'm assuming you have contact with the Young Tribulation Force?"

Natalie nodded.

"When you get home tonight, send them this file. They might be interested in it."

"I want to hear your story," Natalie said.

"Yeah, and I want to hear yours, but not now." Jim sat in front of Peacekeeper Vesario's computer and worked at the keyboard. "Watch the door."

After a few minutes Dekker jotted some notes and stood. "I won't be able to key in the orders from my computer. You'll have to do it from here."

"And we'll be able to get all of them out?"

"Who's down there?"

Natalie listed the four believers she knew. Jim frowned when she mentioned Zeke. "The Zuckermandel guy is off-limits. The others are low enough priority that it might work, but we'll have to work together."

"That means Zeke will have to choose between taking the mark or facing the guillotine."

Jim nodded. "You talked with him. He say anything about it?"

"He said he was ready to take a stand." Natalie looked at the floor. "You should have seen him down there. He was telling people about God, and they were mocking him and laughing. But he didn't care."

Jim put a hand on Natalie's shoulder. "I

know it's hard to lose somebody like this. I hate it. But we have to understand that God is in control and he sees the whole picture."

They heard the elevator ding and the voices of several people in the hallway. Jim opened the office door, shoved Natalie out, and closed it quickly behind them. He whispered, "I'll be in touch soon. Find a way into one of these offices and get the password to the computer." Jim turned and headed for the stairwell as Peacekeeper Vesario came toward them.

Natalie went back to her desk and slipped the computer disk Jim had given her into her purse. She couldn't wait to send the file to the kids in Wisconsin and tell them they had a new friend.

Judd found an e-mail from Chang early one morning and shared it with Lionel and Westin.

> *Judd,*
> *So far nothing has changed about my position with the GC. Perhaps I can hack into their computers and give myself a deadly disease so they won't want me. (My sister is worried, but I am hopeful.)*

> *I'm very sorry about my father's actions
> toward you. I continue to pray that he will
> understand the truth soon. I won't give up
> on him or my mother until they actually
> take the mark.*
> C. W.

"He'd better hurry," Westin said.

"Why?" Judd said.

Westin sighed. "Z-Van talked with one of
the GC heavyweights last night about his
Israel performances."

"There's going to be more than one?"
Lionel said.

Westin nodded. "His contact told him the
loyalty contraptions—I call them head chop-
pers—are already being sent around the
world. They're going to start applying the
marks on prisoners to make sure there are no
glitches. Then GC employees get a chance.
New hires are first in line."

Judd rubbed his forehead. Their time to
give the message to people was running out.

Vicki was thrilled when Natalie told her
about Jim Dekker. She put her head on the
desk and thanked God for his mercy and
provision for their safety. When Vicki tried

to download the file Natalie sent, the computer seemed to lock up.

"No, it's retrieving it," Mark said, watching the progress. "It's huge. Wonder what's on it."

Vicki composed a message to Natalie as she waited. Mark went to another room and pulled the file up on a different computer.

The kids had settled into a routine in Wisconsin, helping Colin and his wife, Becky. They all slept in the underground hideout, girls in beds in one room, boys in sleeping bags in another. Everyone seemed to be adjusting well except Charlie, who took long walks in the countryside each morning and evening. Vicki tried to assure him that the kids would do everything possible for Bo and Ginny, but Charlie didn't seem to believe her.

When Vicki relayed the information Natalie had sent about Jim Dekker and the plan for Bo and Ginny, Charlie's face lit up. "Do you think they'll be able to come here?"

Vicki smiled. "If Natalie and Jim think it's best, they'll be sleeping in the next room."

Mark seemed out of breath as his voice sounded over the intercom. "Could everybody come to the first-floor computer room?"

Mark stood in front of the screen, his hands in his pockets, as the kids gathered. Colin and Becky were there as well. Charlie scooted close to the monitor and tried to look around Mark.

"I suppose it was enough that this Jim Dekker altered the satellite record and saved us all," Mark said. "But he didn't stop there. He's been working on this program for a while. First, take a look at the note he sent."

Mark dragged the letter from the smaller screen to the larger one at the front of the room.

> To: *The Young Trib Force*
> Fr: *Jim Dekker, GC Satellite*
> *Department, Illinois*
> Re: *The Cube*
>
> *I've been watching you guys for a while and have admired your work. That stunt with Damosa and the satellite school was priceless.*
>
> *You might wonder what a guy like me has to do in his spare time. Well, this is it. I've been working on it since I came to know God and started reading Tsion Ben-Judah's Web site.*
>
> *I thought we could use a simple way to explain the truth about God that used more than words. This may be too late, but I think God wants me to give this to you guys and let you go wild with it.*

If you don't think it's a good idea or if there's something wrong with the presentation, trash it. I don't want to give bad information.

If you like it, feel free to send it out and duplicate it anyway you'd like. You can print it, put it on a digital assistant, even load it to your watch. I call it The Cube because of the Dynamic Hologram Projection.

God bless you all.

J. D.

"Let's see it!" Charlie said.

Mark clicked a small icon of a cross with a 3 over the upper right quadrant and the program spun to life. The screen went blank, then projected a 3-D image of a cube in midair. A man floated to the bottom of the cube and Scripture appeared underneath.

"The program runs with or without the text," Mark said. "If you e-mail it to someone, you can leave the text on or off."

The man clutched his chest, and thorns grew around him. The scene represented sin and its hold on every person. The text of Romans 3:23 scrolled into view, "For all have sinned; all fall short of God's glorious standard."

A white shape hovered over the man's

body. "For the wages of sin is death, . . ." The image dissolved into a bright light. Then a hand reaching out filled the cube. ". . . but the free gift of God is eternal life through Christ Jesus our Lord."

The hand turned and Vicki gasped as a nail pierced the flesh. The image enlarged and pulled back, revealing a man on a cross at the top of a hill. The image rotated, giving the kids the entire scope of the scene. "For God so loved the world that he gave his only Son, so that everyone who believes in him will not perish but have eternal life."

The cube went dark, then slowly lightened to show the entrance to a tomb. The murdered man on the cross appeared in the opening and stretched out a hand which grew larger until the nail print became visible.

Finally, images of judgments the earth had suffered since the disappearances flashed. The earthquake, locust-demons, fiery hail, a meteor crashing into the ocean, and people dying.

"These judgments have been given by God so that each person might find the truth that is Jesus Christ," the text said. "Without him, we perish. With him, we have eternal life."

More verses were listed along with a prayer to receive the gift of God. The 3-D image of the cross swirled and came to rest on a lonely hill, and the cube went blank.

The room fell silent and Vicki wiped away a tear. Everyone seemed moved by the presentation.

"What do you think?" Mark said.

"How soon can we send it?" Conrad said.

TEN

Fortunato Speaks

VICKI and the others began work immediately with The Cube. They set up an e-mail database of every person who had ever contacted their Web site. Vicki helped separate believers from unbelievers and e-mailed an explanation and the file to the believers first.

This is a tool to use with your family, friends, and anyone you think needs to understand the message, Vicki wrote.

Shelly was in charge of finding any angry or threatening e-mails. They would eventually send The Cube to everyone, but they didn't want to contact loyal Global Community followers and have them post warnings.

By the next day, response was pouring in. One girl in Greece wrote, *I've been trying to explain what I believe to my family for so long. The Cube helped show them God's love. My family hasn't prayed yet, but I'm not giving up. Thanks for your work.*

A teenage boy from California reported that he showed The Cube to a few friends and they were blown away by the holographics. *I kept the text off when I played it and they had no idea what it meant. When I read the verses, a couple of them understood and prayed. I'm still working on the others.*

Colin Dial walked in smiling. "I just talked with my friend who helped me find this equipment. I told him what Dekker created, and he's found a truckload of some personal digital organizers. You could give one of those to a person on the street if you want, or pull it out and use it as you're talking with someone."

"I just saw a report about the satellite schools," Conrad said. "They're starting up again. We could pass those gadgets out to people going inside."

Mark talked with Natalie by phone late one night and worked throughout the day to hack into the Global Community's computers. With Conrad's help, he finally made it inside and found important information, including a drawing of Carpathia's mark.

Vicki spent most of her time at the computer answering e-mails. She was excited to open a note from Tsion Ben-Judah. He wrote that the adult Tribulation Force had found a safe hiding place, and he was busy teaching converts around the world.

> *I would especially appreciate your prayers about a sensitive matter in the Force. Things happen when you young people pray, I know it, so please ask God to give us wisdom in the coming days.*
>
> *If I am right, Antichrist will pour out his wrath against my believing countrymen soon. Someone will need to lead them to safety. This person will be a modern-day Moses, fleeing an evil ruler and taking his people to a safe haven.*
>
> *Pray this person will have confidence that God can work in him and communicate through him far beyond any ability he ever had before. He will have to oppose Antichrist himself and rally the masses to do what is right.*
>
> *Thank you for praying. I ask that each of you will be strengthened inwardly for the difficult days ahead.*

Vicki posted the letter in different rooms of the hideout. Charlie asked what Vicki thought was going to happen in Israel.

"What do you think?" Vicki said.

Charlie scratched his head. "I've been

trying to figure it out. I think Nicolae is going to break his promise about protecting Israel and do something in the Jewish temple." He scowled. "What does *defile* mean?"

"It means you take something good, something holy, and mess it up really bad."

"How do you know big words like that?"

Vicki smiled. "I had to look that one up myself. What else do you think's going to happen?"

"Nicolae is really mad at Jewish people. God doesn't want him to hurt them, so he's got a hiding place. This person Dr. Ben-Judah wrote about is going to lead them to it, and I think I know who it is."

"Who?"

"Well, he has to be Jewish, and he has to be a believer. I'd expect he'd have to be able to speak well enough to get people to follow him. Sounds like Dr. Ben-Judah to me."

"You might be right," Vicki said. "Tsion teaches that God's people will be supernaturally protected."

"What does that mean?"

"Do you remember back before the disappearances when Israel was attacked?"

"You mean all the bombs that fell but didn't kill anybody?"

Vicki nodded. "I think God and his angels will protect them."

Charlie looked at the floor and sighed. "I wish Phoenix was supernaturally protected."

"Is that why you've been so down?"

Charlie nodded. "You promised Ryan you'd take care of his dog, and I took that seriously."

Vicki put a hand on Charlie's shoulder. "It's not that I don't take it seriously. I know Ryan wouldn't have wanted us to put ourselves in danger. I actually think Phoenix was trying to save us in some way. He must have sensed the danger."

Charlie nodded. "I wish I knew what happened to him."

Natalie Bishop watched the communication between Deputy Commander Henderson and his superiors. The man seemed in a frenzy meeting with high-level officials. Natalie wondered if Henderson's job was on the line, but she didn't dare ask.

One afternoon Henderson called her into his office. "Is something wrong, sir?" she said.

"No, I just thought I'd let you in on your new assignment. Command asked me to ID people from different levels to participate in an upcoming exercise."

"You're moving me?"

"No, I recommended you represent Morale Monitors at the processing of the first group taking the mark of loyalty. You'll observe at the GC compound in Wheaton."

Natalie felt faint. She put a hand to her head and gasped.

Henderson put a hand on her shoulder. "I know it's an honor, Bishop. And you've earned it."

"When does it begin?"

"Only a couple more days and you'll be able to wear the mark of your lord and your god."

I already do, Natalie thought.

Judd didn't hear more from Chang for a few days and worried that something might have gone wrong. Finally, Chang wrote that he had been able to avoid meeting with the GC, but that his father continued to insist he work for Carpathia.

Judd outlined a plan for Chang to get away from his parents' apartment and hide on Z-Van's plane. Westin would meet him at the airport and make sure he made it safely. He would hide there until the trip to Israel. Mr. Stein and Sam Goldberg had agreed to help find Chang a place to stay.

Chang agreed but asked that Judd and his friends wait. Chang said he had spoken with another believer on the inside of the Global Community who was also trying to help.

Z-Van called everyone in the suite together, which now included more members of his band and his agent, Cyril Bernard. The man had rushed to New Babylon after seeing Z-Van's surprise press conference, but Z-Van had refused to see him until now. Cyril dressed in colorful clothes and huge glasses. His shoes sparkled and he smelled of too much cologne.

"This project is going to be, without a doubt, the greatest album in the history of modern recording," Cyril said in his heavy British accent. "It represents the two greatest comebacks—"

Z-Van rolled his eyes and said, "Shut up!"

"I was speaking of yours and His Excellency's, of course."

Z-Van slurred his words and appeared to sway as he talked. He stood between Judd and Lionel, put an arm around each, and introduced them as the reason for his miraculous comeback. "If my music brings joy or causes people to worship the true and risen lord, you can thank these two young people."

Judd glanced at Lionel, and it was all the two of them could do not to run from the room. Z-Van's breath smelled terrible, and he hung on the boys like an old coat.

"I'm sure these two have wondered why I've let them stay so long. The truth is, they tried to convince me their religion was right and I didn't buy it. Now I'm trying to convince them that the potentate is lord."

"As if anyone would need convincing of that," Cyril muttered.

"If they haven't been persuaded yet, perhaps being in the audience today when the second in command speaks will convince them."

"You mean we're going to meet Reverend Fortunato?" Cyril interrupted.

"Not Reverend," Z-Van said. "Most High Reverend."

Later, Judd and Lionel looked for a way out as the group walked along together. It was noon in New Babylon and the temperature felt a lot like the day of Nicolae's resurrection. Tourists still walked the grounds near the palace with cameras, gawking and pointing at anyone they thought might be famous.

Two GC Peacekeepers ushered the group inside the vast church of Carpathianism. Judd and the others were seated near the front, at the right of the podium that seemed to hover high above the audience. When the time came, a velvet curtain parted and Fortunato emerged, wearing a long red-and-blue robe.

The Most High Reverend reported on the race to complete duplicates of Carpathia's image. Live interviews with people at different locations around the globe showed the progress, but none had as many as the United Carpathian States.

Some statues were black, many made of gold, some crystal. When the screen showed an orange replica of Carpathia, Lionel leaned over to Judd. "I wonder if that one comes without pulp."

Judd snickered and Cyril elbowed him.

Fortunato relayed the sad news that Jerusalem had failed to begin the building process of their statue. He looked into the camera and scowled. "Speaking under the authority of the risen potentate, I say woe! Woe and beware to the enemies of the lord of this globe who would thumb their noses in the face of the most high!"

Just as quickly, he was back in his gentle mode, speaking as if he were tucking them all in bed for a bedtime story. He reminded everyone that he had been given power to call down fire from heaven on the unfaithful, but that Carpathia was full of love and forgiveness.

"Yeah, right," Lionel whispered.

"One week from today, the object of our adoration shall personally visit his children in Jerusalem. He will be there not only to deal with those who oppose him—for he is, besides being a loving god, a just god—but also to bless and accept worship and praise from the citizens otherwise without voice.

"As your global pastor, let me urge those in Jerusalem who are loyal to their lord and king to bravely show your support to the one worthy of all honor and glory when he arrives in your home city. May it be a triumphal entry like none before it."

Fortunato promised safety for anyone who would worship Carpathia in the presence of Judah-ites and Orthodox Jews. "Unless they see the error of their ways and come on bent knee to beg forgiveness of their lord, new leadership will be in place before His Excellency leaves that great city.

"And to those who swear that the temple is off-limits to the potentate himself, I say, dare not come against the army of the lord of hosts. He is a god of peace and reconciliation, but thou shalt have no other gods before him. There shall not be erected or allowed to stand any house of worship anywhere on this planet that does not recognize His Excellency as its sole object of devotion. Nicolae Carpathia, the potentate, is risen!"

The crowd assembled rose with a cry of "He is risen indeed," but Judd and Lionel half stood, half sat.

"All statues must be completed within two days and should be open for worship. And, as you know, the first one hundred cities with finished and approved units will be the first to be awarded loyalty mark application centers."

Fortunato showed a replay of his calling fire from heaven and Carpathia's rising from the dead. Judd shuddered. This, along with recorded messages from Carpathia and Fortunato, would be shown at each mark application facility.

Fortunato addressed the possibility of counterfeit marks. "While it may be impossible for any but highly skilled and trained observers to tell a fake mark from the real, biochip scanners cannot be fooled."

Judd glanced at Lionel and winced. The screen switched to a shot of a guillotine, and Fortunato laughed. "I can't imagine any citizen of the Global Community having to worry about such a device, unless he or she is still in the cult of the Judah-ites or Orthodox Judaism."

The Most High Reverend showed the

world a stack of applications from people who wanted to be first to show their loyalty to Carpathia. Judd noticed Z-Van squirm in his chair like a child grasping at a new toy.

"Does the application hurt? It does not. With technology so advanced and local anesthesia so effective, you will feel only the pressure of the biochip inserter. By the time any discomfort would have passed, the anesthetic will still be working.

"Bless you, my friends, in the name of our risen lord and master, His Excellency the Potentate, Nicolae Carpathia."

As the crowd rose and applauded Fortunato, Lionel leaned over to Judd. "Chang doesn't have much time."

ELEVEN

The GC Wardrobe

Natalie frantically worked with Jim Dekker to get the believers out of jail, but she became discouraged when she discovered that Zeke Sr. had been moved to the facility in Wheaton. Jim Dekker helped her stay focused on the Shairtons, Maggie, and the newest believer, Manny.

Jim invented a Commander Regis Blakely, who was stationed in Joliet. He e-mailed Deputy Commander Henderson a list of four prisoners he wanted to interrogate before the mark of loyalty was given. If Henderson bought it, Colin Dial would become Commander Blakely and retrieve the four.

Natalie sat outside Henderson's office, waiting for the man's reaction to the e-mail. She heard him curse and slam his fist on the desk.

"Is anything wrong, sir?" Natalie said, sticking her head in the door.

"A commander thinks we're not doing our job," Henderson said. "He wants to interrogate some prisoners."

"Can I help?"

Henderson looked out the window as a document printed. He handed her the page. "Make sure we actually have all four of these people. We'll transport them tomorrow to a holding facility in Joliet."

Vicki and the others in Wisconsin helped clean the Dials' van. They wanted it to look like an official GC vehicle, so the kids scrubbed it clean, inside and out.

Next, Becky Dial brought a printout of the Global Community's insignia and began painting it on both sides of the van. Becky had studied art in college, and when they were finished, Vicki compared the picture with the painting and couldn't tell the difference.

Mark took an emergency call from Natalie, who gave directions to Jim Dekker's home. Dekker had a GC uniform for Colin and instructions for the rescue.

Mark told the others Natalie's plan. Everyone had been excited about The Cube and its success on the Internet, but now they had to concentrate on helping their friends.

"I don't think anyone should go with me," Colin said.

"At least let me tag along in case you need help," Mark said.

"I know how these guys operate," Conrad said. "Let me go."

Mark and Conrad argued until Vicki suggested they flip a coin. Conrad won. The kids circled around and prayed for safety. Vicki turned away as Colin kissed his wife and whispered something to her.

A noise in the distance startled Vicki. Charlie heard it too and ran to the front of the house. When Vicki caught up, she saw something running through a field toward them.

Ears flopping, jaws bouncing, a dog lumbered toward the house.

"Phoenix!" Charlie yelled as he ran toward the animal.

"How could he have found this place?" Mark said.

Vicki smiled. "I've heard of things like this, but I've never seen it happen."

The dog bowled Charlie over, and the two rolled in the grass fifty yards away. When Phoenix made it to the house, everyone took turns petting and hugging him.

Mark and Conrad inspected the dog's collar for a homing device, but found nothing. "From the looks of him, he hasn't eaten in days," Mark said.

Becky ran for some food, and Charlie said he was going to give Phoenix a bath.

"That's a happy ending," Melinda said to Vicki.

Vicki nodded and watched Colin and Conrad get into the van. "We need one more happy ending before this is over."

Conrad stayed out of sight in the back of Colin's van until they found Jim Dekker's address. The farmhouse was in McHenry, a small town in Illinois just south of the Wisconsin border. The earthquake had damaged a grain silo and the barn in the back, but the white house still stood. The porch was screened in just like Conrad remembered from his grandparents' house.

Jim Dekker greeted the two and had them park in the back. The house smelled musty and white sheets covered the furniture. Conrad noticed a rickety piano with yellow keys in the living room. A GC uniform hung from a dusty chandelier in the dining room. Jim took Colin's picture and loaded it into his computer for his new ID badge.

"Where did you get the uniform?" Colin said.

"Satellite operations has its own dry cleaning in the basement. I made a master key that gives me access. While I was on my coffee break last night I borrowed it. We'll need to return it before tomorrow morning."

Colin smiled. "I suppose you made a nameplate for me?"

Jim nodded and pulled off the plastic wrapping. "Believe me, when you meet any Global Community personnel, they'll stop in their tracks and salute."

Conrad explained that he had been a Morale Monitor before becoming a believer. "I've been teaching Colin the correct way to salute."

"Good," Jim said. "Have you had any military experience, Colin?"

Colin shook his head, and Jim gave him a crash course on GC protocol—when to salute, how to talk, and how to treat those lower in rank. "You walk like a top dog, like you're superior. It's all in the attitude."

"I didn't think I was actually going into the building."

"You won't, unless you have to. Natalie says Henderson leaves around 5 P.M. You'll call him just before he leaves and tell him you're in the area with a GC vehicle and would like the prisoners you requested."

"Won't they be suspicious when I don't have a driver?"

Jim pointed at his head and said, "Attitude." He stood, threw out his chest, and said, "Try me."

"Okay, uh, Commander, why are you driving around without a—"

"What business is that of yours, Deputy!" Jim interrupted. "If I want to ride in here on a motor scooter and take these prisoners to the North Pole, you'll salute and go back to your office. Understand?"

Conrad laughed.

"What are you smiling at, kid? Wipe that grin off your face."

Conrad shook his head. "You act like that and we'll be able to bring the whole jail home."

Colin asked why they had to leave Zeke Sr. behind, and Jim explained that the GC wanted to make an example of him. "Natalie says they've even separated him from the rest of the inmates and have a separate guard."

"They think he's going to try and escape?" Conrad said.

"No, Zeke's been telling all the prisoners about God, and the GC is afraid he's having too much influence on them."

Jim brought some food and asked about The Cube.

"Some kids are writing and saying they've been 'cubed' and are going to 'cube' others. It's wild."

While they waited, Conrad asked to hear Jim's story. Jim said he would try to give the short version. Jim had grown up in Glen Ellyn, a suburb west of Chicago. "My mom and dad were Christians and took us kids to church every week. I have three older sisters.

"I was into computers, biology, and read a lot of science fiction. Big horror fan. Any movie that was supposed to scare you and I was there. I wanted to go to Northwestern, had the grades too, but it was just too much money for my parents, so I settled for a state school."

"Did your parents know you weren't a Christian?" Conrad said.

Jim nodded. "I'm sure. I'd argue with them about evolution and creation. They sat me down one night and said they were concerned about the direction I was headed, but I blew them off. I wasn't a bad kid. I didn't do drugs or run around. In fact, that was what kept me from really knowing God."

"What do you mean?"

"I never really thought I was that bad a

person. I didn't need God. I didn't even believe he existed. I went to church, sat in the Sunday school classes, closed my eyes when people prayed. I even took notes during the sermon sometimes. Other kids played the good-Christian routine, then went out and partied, but I didn't. I figured if there was a God, he'd be okay with me if I just did what my parents told me.

"I signed up for the military after college and they put me into a specialized unit that used satellite technology. I had a blast. When I got out, I was hired by a computer company developing advanced search-and-destroy technology. Stuff in fighter jets and helicopters."

"That's how you knew how to make The Cube!"

Jim smiled and nodded. "I had talked with my dad one evening about his health. He wasn't feeling well and my mom was worried. He said he was proud of me for all I had accomplished, but that the most important thing was whether I truly knew Jesus. He told me the Lord was coming back and that I needed to be ready."

"What did you say?"

"I didn't want to upset him so I just told him he didn't have to worry, that I'd made my peace with God." Jim leaned forward, elbows on knees, and shook his head. "That night it happened. People I'd known all my life disappeared. I heard about it the next morning and drove over to my parents' house. There were people in the streets, confused, crying, looking for their babies. I walked inside the house and a sound scared me to death."

"What was it?"

"Silence. In all my years growing up, Mom and Dad had played a Christian radio station. It was on all through the night. You couldn't walk into that living room without hearing a Christian song or some teaching from the Bible. That morning it was like somebody had sucked the life right out of that place.

"I found their nightclothes in bed and a bunch of medication on the nightstand next to my dad's side, along with his Bible. Dad had a little notebook underneath that he used to write out prayers for his kids. Before he fell asleep that night, he had written something about me."

Jim went out of the room and returned with a dog-eared spiral notebook. He opened it and handed it to Conrad. Colin leaned in close to see. The handwriting was scrawled across the page and hard to read:

> *Father, I pray again for Jimmy tonight and ask that you would open the eyes of his*

heart so that he would know the hope you want him to have. He doesn't know about the riches of the inheritance he could have or the great power of your strength that can work so mightily in him. I pray that you would take off the blinders and help him see how much you love him. Jimmy could do such great things for you if he would only give his heart to you. Show him the truth. In Jesus' name, amen.

Jim looked out the window to the back of the farm. "I found about a dozen of those notebooks on the shelf in his closet. Every one of them had pages and pages of prayers for me. That one was taken from Ephesians. He didn't know it, but his prayers were answered that morning by his bed. I called out to God and prayed I wasn't too late."

"What about your sisters?" Colin said.

Jim shook his head. "All three of them were gone, with their families. I was alone. For a long time I thought it was hopeless, that I'd just missed out. Then I started reading the Bible and trying to understand the things I had heard all my life. You can't believe how relieved I was when I started reading about others who had prayed and had been forgiven. Then Tsion Ben-Judah came out with his findings about prophecy, and I knew I had to work on the inside of the Global Community to help people."

Jim asked them to follow him, and the three descended the musty stairs to the basement. "Over the past few months I've been able to set up a bunch of names for made-up GC soldiers and workers. I knew I'd have to have more than just names to make them look real."

Jim switched on the light and Conrad gasped. Racks of GC uniforms lined the walls. He had everything from Morale Monitor to Peacekeeper outfits, both male and female.

"We should be able to find something for you, if you want to be the commander's driver," Jim said to Conrad.

"How did you get all these?"

"I got the idea right after the earthquake. I knew there would be a lot of GC bodies with the coming judgments, so I found a believer at a funeral home who was handling the bodies. He agreed to get me as many uniforms as he could sneak out. I don't own any higher rank than a deputy commander."

After Jim had given final instructions, he handed Colin a cell phone. "This is yours, Commander."

Conrad drove the van and followed Jim toward Des Plaines.

Colin sat in the passenger seat buttoning his commander's uniform. "You ready for this, Morale Monitor?" he said in a deep voice.

"Yes, sir."

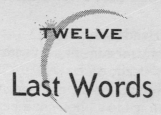

TWELVE

Last Words

NATALIE watched the clock at the jail and prayed that Colin would arrive soon. From her access to the GC computer she saw that Deputy Commander Henderson had approved the transfer of the prisoners for early the next morning.

Henderson approached his secretary and asked her to contact Commander Blakely's office in Joliet. Natalie's heart sank. "Is there anything I can help you with, sir?"

Henderson shook his head. "Something's weird about this Blakely. I'd never heard of him before yesterday, and neither has anybody else around here."

Henderson's secretary buzzed him. "I've found Commander Blakely in the database, but no one can tell me how to reach him in Joliet."

"Odd," Henderson said.

"Check the message he sent with the transfer order," Natalie said.

Henderson pulled the message up, and Natalie pointed to a phone number at the bottom of the screen. Henderson punched his speakerphone and dialed. The phone rang twice, and then a man with a deep voice answered gruffly, "Blakely."

Henderson sat up straight. "Uh, Commander, sir, this is Deputy Commander Henderson in Des Plaines."

"Yeah, glad you called. You get my transfer order processed?"

"Yes, sir, we'll transport them tomorrow."

"Don't bother. I'm headed your way now. I'll pick them up myself."

"But, sir, I thought we were supposed to—"

"Hey, tough break with those Judah-ites who got away. I'm hoping one of these will break and tell us what we want to know."

"Well, sir, the Hispanic prisoner, Aguilara, isn't charged with sedition. He's here on a gang charge—"

"Yeah, but I understand you had him in proximity to the gas station owner, was it Zuckermandel?"

"Yes, but he is in solitary now and—"

"We're pulling up to your place now. You bring 'em out and I'll wait here."

Henderson looked at Natalie and mouthed, "He's here."

"You want me to have the guards bring the prisoners outside?" Natalie said.

"You got that, Henderson?" the deep-voiced man said.

"Yes, sir, we'll be right out."

Henderson phoned the guard station and asked that the four be brought to the front parking lot immediately. Natalie tagged along, not wanting to miss the exchange.

Henderson walked through sliding doors into the sunshine. A GC van was parked near the entrance. Commander Blakely stepped out and Henderson saluted. The commander returned the salute and handed him official-looking papers.

Henderson scanned the documents. "We had planned to bring the prisoners to you in Joliet tomorrow."

"I appreciate that. Truth is, I'm part of a covert division looking into the Judah-ites. I'm hoping for new information from these prisoners."

"You don't think we've been lax in our questioning, do you?"

The commander held up a hand. "This has

nothing to do with your hard work, Henderson. As a matter of fact, your name came up in a joint conference we held the other day."

"Me, sir?"

"Nobody envies where you are. It's a real hotbed of rebel activity."

Henderson nodded. "I had wondered what the upper brass thought of my situation."

Commander Blakely hesitated as the prisoners were led outside. The guard handed a key to the Morale Monitor driving the van.

"When will you begin applying the mark of loyalty?" Blakely said.

"I'm headed to observe another facility in the morning. We hope to start here tomorrow afternoon."

"Good," Blakely said. "Now, if you'll excuse us, we'll take care of these prisoners. And I'll put in a good word for you at command. You've been very helpful."

As the commander drove away, he tipped his hat to Natalie, showing the mark of the true believer. She smiled and saluted.

When Conrad had driven a few minutes from Des Plaines, he sighed and pulled to the side of the road. Colin released their new friends from their shackles.

"That was quite a performance back there," Maggie Carlson said, slapping Colin on the shoulder.

Jim Dekker pulled in behind them and climbed in. He greeted the four former prisoners and took his cell phone from Colin. Everyone agreed to meet at Jim's house in McHenry before heading to Wisconsin. "Stay in character, Commander, and keep going."

Vicki and the others whooped and yelled when they heard the news from Conrad. Becky Dial quickly brought some new cots and sleeping bags out of the storage area and prepared for the new arrivals.

After Fortunato's speech, Judd and Lionel had kept their distance from Z-Van's crowd and slipped back to the hotel with Westin. After conferring, they decided they would call Chang that evening and tell him of the escape plan.

Judd dialed Chang's number and Mrs. Wong answered. "He not talk now."

"Please, I really need to talk with him."

The phone clunked on the table, and the

woman said something in Chinese. Mr. Wong picked up. "You the one have dinner with us?"

"Yes, sir, I just wanted—"

"You not good influence on my son. You stop calling. No more. Understand?"

Mr. Wong slammed the phone down and Judd hung up. He turned to Lionel and Westin. "I don't like the sound of that. Mr. Wong's really angry."

"You think he knows Chang's a believer?" Lionel said.

Judd shook his head and tried e-mailing Chang again, but there was no response.

"Okay, that's enough for me," Westin said. "New plan. The plane's ready. All we have to do is contact Chang and take him there. The question is, how?"

"We could just go in and get him," Lionel said.

"Too much security," Judd said. "Only way in is through the front door and GC guards check IDs."

"They can't keep him inside forever," Lionel said.

"Good thinking," Judd said. "We'll set up watch outside the building and if Chang comes out alone, we'll grab him and head for the plane. If he's with his parents, we can follow them and wait until he goes into a bathroom or something."

Lionel and Westin agreed, and Judd described Chang to them. Lionel volunteered for the first watch, and Judd walked him to the GC building. It was getting late and most of the lights were out in the apartments above them. Lionel found a spot behind some shrubbery where he could see the front door.

"That's the only door I've seen anybody coming through," Judd said. "I think they have to check in and out with the guard."

A new guard for the next shift walked past. When the man had gone into the building, Judd patted Lionel on the back and told him to call if he saw anything. "I'll be back at about five in the morning."

Natalie's joy at the release of the four believers was short-lived. The next morning she accompanied an excited Deputy Commander Henderson and a number of other Peacekeepers to the former DuPage County Jail. It was now the main holding area for criminals in the Midwest.

The jail buzzed with activity as workers prepared for the application of Carpathia's mark. The group was led to a room specially created at the entrance to the cellblock. Prisoners were to be taken one by one to the "loyalty application room" and given their biochip injection and identifying mark.

Natalie asked a woman she knew where the guillotine was and the woman frowned. "You're not supposed to use that word. It's 'loyalty enforcement facilitator.' "

"Right," Natalie said. "Where is it?"

"They won't need it. I mean, who in their right mind would choose death instead of a little injection and a tattoo?"

Natalie wanted to tell the woman the truth. This was more than simply numbering people for identification. Any person who willingly took the mark of Carpathia would seal their eternal destiny. "In case there is somebody who's that stupid, where would they do it?" Natalie said instead.

The woman pointed to the top of the stairs. "They're putting it together in one of the interrogation rooms. But don't get your hopes up."

Deputy Commander Henderson had seemed happier since meeting Commander Blakely. He spoke with a friend he knew at the facility and assured the man his job wasn't in jeopardy.

When they completed the tour, Henderson adjusted his dress uniform and motioned everyone outside. "It's show time, people."

Cameras and microphones covered the

lawn outside the jail. A slight breeze swept through as GC employees gathered in a semi-circle behind the cameras. The head of the facility introduced himself and made a short statement.

A reporter asked, "Sir, do you expect any executions today?"

The man smiled. "We have seen the leader of our world rise from the dead. Who could say no to this man? All he asks is that we identify ourselves with his cause, the cause of peace."

When the press conference was over, Natalie and the others returned to the loyalty application room. The crowd was so large at first that she had to stand at the top of the stairs to watch prisoners being led in. Two women were shown in first, surprised at all the onlookers. After what seemed like only a minute, the procedure was over. The crowd applauded and gawked at the insignia both women had chosen.

Natalie was able to move closer after the first few prisoners were processed. One man held the injection device for the biochip and two other officers were in charge of the tattoo. They worked like machines, turning out followers of Carpathia like sausages.

Each person was asked a simple question

when they entered the room. "Are you ready to show your loyalty to His Excellency?"

Most simply said, "Yes," but one man muttered, "What choice do I have?"

It was after noon and Natalie still hadn't seen Zeke Sr. Her heart leapt when she heard one worker say, "That's the last of them."

Deputy Commander Henderson checked the list and said, "What about Zucker-mandel?"

Natalie climbed halfway up the stairs and listened to the echo of footsteps down the corridor. Zeke Sr. stood tall as he walked the length of the hall. Natalie wondered if she would have the strength to watch.

"Are you ready to show your loyalty to His Excellency?" a guard said.

"I sure am," Zeke said.

"Where do you want the mark, on the fore-head or the hand?"

"You can keep it. I'm showing loyalty to the real Potentate—God. And I'm not taking your mark or your injection."

Silence. Deputy Commander Henderson stepped forward. "You know what this means, you old fool?"

"I'm not the fool. People who take this mark are because—"

A slap, then Zeke crumpled to the floor. Natalie wanted to cry out, but she held her tongue. A guard hustled Zeke upstairs and Henderson followed close behind. Natalie couldn't move as Zeke was pushed past her. A door closed around the corner.

Natalie managed to climb to the top of the stairs. She slipped inside a nearby observation room, where she could see what was happening through the one-way glass. Zeke stood by the guillotine, blood trickling from his mouth.

Henderson pointed at the guillotine. "You will not make a mockery of this process. Will you take the mark?!"

Zeke spoke slowly through gritted teeth. "I . . . will . . . not."

Two guards pulled him to his knees while Henderson raised the blade to its full height. Zeke's lips moved in silent prayer as the guards cuffed him. The old man leaned forward until his head fit through the opening.

"You have one final chance," Henderson said.

Natalie put a hand to her face and trembled. She wanted to rush into the room, mace all the guards, and release Zeke. Everything in her screamed out to help, but there was nothing she could do.

"Father," Zeke said, "I pray you'd forgive these people for what they're about to do.

Help them see the truth. Jesus Christ is the true Lord of the universe. He alone deserves to be worshiped."

Deputy Commander Henderson raised a hand, and the guard beside the machine reached for a lever. Zeke whispered, "Into your hands I commit my spirit."

Natalie turned away at the sound of the falling blade. She crumpled onto the floor of the darkened room and wept. As workers removed the lifeless body, she cried for Zeke. She cried for the other believers around the world who would have to endure the same punishment. And she cried for herself.

ABOUT THE AUTHORS

Jerry B. Jenkins (www.jerryjenkins.com) is the writer of the Left Behind series. He owns the Jerry B. Jenkins Christian Writers Guild, an organization dedicated to mentoring aspiring authors. Former vice president for publishing for the Moody Bible Institute of Chicago, he also served many years as editor of *Moody* magazine and is now Moody's writer-at-large.

His writing has appeared in publications as varied as *Reader's Digest, Parade, Guideposts,* in-flight magazines, and dozens of other periodicals. Jenkins's biographies include books with Billy Graham, Hank Aaron, Bill Gaither, Luis Palau, Walter Payton, Orel Hershiser, and Nolan Ryan, among many others. His books appear regularly on the *New York Times, USA Today, Wall Street Journal,* and *Publishers Weekly* bestseller lists.

Jerry is also the writer of the nationally syndicated sports story comic strip *Gil Thorp,* distributed to newspapers across the United States by Tribune Media Services.

Jerry and his wife, Dianna, live in Colorado and have three grown sons.

Dr. Tim LaHaye (www.timlahaye.com), who conceived the idea of fictionalizing an account of the Rapture and the Tribulation, is a noted author, minister, and nationally recognized speaker on Bible prophecy. He is the founder of both Tim LaHaye Ministries and The PreTrib Research Center. He also recently cofounded the Tim LaHaye School of Prophecy at Liberty University. Presently Dr. LaHaye speaks at many of the major Bible prophecy conferences in the U.S. and Canada, where his current prophecy books are very popular.

Dr. LaHaye holds a doctor of ministry degree from Western Theological Seminary and a doctor of literature degree from Liberty University. For twenty-five years he pastored one of the nation's outstanding churches in San Diego, which grew to three locations. It was during that time that he founded two accredited Christian high schools, a Christian school system of ten schools, and Christian Heritage College.

Dr. LaHaye has written over forty books that have been published in more than thirty languages. He has written books on a wide variety of subjects, such as family life, temperaments, and Bible prophecy. His current fiction works, the Left Behind series, written with Jerry B. Jenkins, continue to appear on the best-seller lists of the Christian Booksellers Association, *Publishers Weekly*, *Wall Street Journal*, *USA Today*, and the *New York Times*.

He is the father of four grown children and grandfather of nine. Snow skiing, waterskiing, motorcycling, golfing, vacationing with family, and jogging are among his leisure activities.

The Future Is Clear

Check out the exciting Left Behind: The Kids series

BOOKS #29 AND #30 COMING SOON!

Discover the latest about the Left Behind series and complete line of products at

www.leftbehind.com

Hooked on the exciting
Left Behind: The Kids series?
Then you'll love the dramatic audios!

Listen as the characters come to life in this theatrical
audio that makes the saga of those left behind
even more exciting.

High-tech sound effects, original music,
and professional actors will have you
on the edge of your seat.

Experience the heart-stopping action and
suspense of the end times for yourself!

Three exciting volumes available on CD or cassette.